PURRFECT CUT

THE MYSTERIES OF MAX 14

NIC SAINT

PUSS IN PRINT PUBLICATIONS

PURRFECT CUT

The Mysteries of Max 14

Copyright © 2019 by Nic Saint

Edited by Chereese Graves

www.nicsaint.com

Give feedback on the book at: info@nicsaint.com

facebook.com/nicsaintauthor
@nicsaintauthor

First Edition

Printed in the U.S.A

CHAPTER 1

A bashful sun was playing peekaboo over the horizon and distributing its first timid rays upon a restful world when I woke up. As usual I'd been dozing at the foot of my human's bed after having spent the first part of the night exploring the ultimate range of my singing voice. As you may or may not know, I've long been a member of Hampton Cove's cat choir, pride of our small town, where cats can still be cats and sing their little hearts out. Only Shanille, our stalwart and earnest conductor, had recently kicked me out of the choir, on account of the fact that several of the members had complained about my abject failure to carry a tune. The incident had greatly saddened me, as you can well imagine, since I've always been a staunch proponent of cats' rights to express themselves in song. So when my membership card was withdrawn I must confess it shook me to the very core of my being.

Fortunately I'm not the kind of cat who takes life's vicissitudes lying down, so to speak, even though ironically enough I do spend a great portion of my life lying down, and soon I was practicing hard to make a triumphant return.

Last night offered me the first opportunity since returning from England, where my human's adventures had taken us, to showcase my progress. And to my elation Shanille and the other members—even those whose complaints had terminated my contract in the first place—deemed me fit for duty once more.

So it was with renewed fervor that I rejoined the choir's rank and file, and I won't conceal the fact that the whole thing gave me a distinct sense that all was well in my world, and upon ending last night's rehearsal, I practically skipped along the road, extremely pleased with myself and my progress.

It isn't too much to say that the mood was festive, so my friends and I decided to paint this small town of ours red, and Brutus led us along all of his favorite haunts, like a nice little rooftop restaurant that keeps the bins out where we can reach them, and our gang of four—myself, Dooley, Harriet and of course Brutus—experienced an enjoyable night on the town. It was only understandable, then, that I felt the need to sleep in. It was with a slight sense of annoyance, therefore, that I greeted the rising sun, which had decided to cut my extended slumber short by spreading its light across a peaceful world.

I stretched and yawned cavernously, as is my habit, and glanced around in search of Dooley, who usually likes to fall asleep next to me. Once upon a time we used to have a big chunk of the bed all to ourselves, but that was before Odelia decided to hook up with a burly policeman who answers to the name Chase Kingsley, and asked him to move in with her. Nowadays the bed is a little cramped for two humans and two cats, which tends to create a touch of awkwardness. The issue isn't Odelia, who's a fairly shortish human being, so her feet don't invade the stretch of bed I like to call my own. What's more, she tends to curl up into a ball when she sleeps—the fetus position I think experts like to call it—which adds to my acreage. No, the problem is Chase, who's one of those long and stretchy humans, and likes to stick his feet where they don't belong: in our territory. I've mentioned this to Odelia, and she's promised to have a talk with the invasive cop, but until then it's tough for a cat to find the space to sleep in peace. Especially since Chase is not one of your more peaceful sleepers. The man tends to toss and turn, and even lash out when the mood strikes, giving poor Dooley the occasional kick in the tail end.

I guess scientists who claim that people sleeping in separate beds enjoy a deeper, better sleep are on to something. All I know is that if only Chase would sleep in a separate bed, we'd all be better off—or at least I would.

Yes, I know I can always sleep on the couch, and I also know there are several other spots at my disposal. Like Marge and Tex's bed. But Odelia's parents' bed is already spoken for, by Brutus and Harriet, and even they have confided in me they suffer the same fate Dooley and I do, with Tex being one of those stringbeany types, whose highly-strung feet seem to have a mind of their own. Dooley, of course, is in the best position of all: he can choose to sleep at Odelia's, or Grandma's. Why he chooses Odelia's is beyond me. She's not technically his human, and still he spends all of his nights here. Then again, it's comforting to have my best friend and wingman nearby, and perhaps he feels the same way, which is why he endures Chase's nervous footwork, and so do I.

I opened one eye, then the other, and saw that Odelia was awake already. Oddly enough she was staring at Chase, who was still fast asleep. So I elbowed Dooley in the tummy and he muttered something that didn't sound entirely friendly.

"Check this out," I whispered. "Odelia is making a study of Chase."

Dooley reluctantly dragged his heavy eyelids open and stared in the direction indicated.

"Huh," he said finally. "Weird."

"Right?"

We both watched on as Odelia watched, with a strange look on her face, the sleeping cop.

"I don't get it," said Dooley. "What's the big attraction?"

"I have no idea," I confessed.

"It's just a sleeping human."

"It is, and he's not even looking his best."

Chase, who some people claim is a handsome fellow, with one of those chiseled faces, strong jaws and long, brown hair, doesn't look his best in the morning. His trademark mane is usually tousled, and more often than not there's a tiny thread of drool visibly at the corner of his mouth. Not exactly the kind of face that would successfully grace the cover of a romance novel. Then again, Odelia's features aren't much to write home about either. Her fair hair is usually a mess, and she develops weird sleep marks on her fine-boned face.

"I mean, if you've seen one sleeping human, you've seen them all," I said.

"It's love," suddenly a third party entered the discussion.

Dooley and I looked up in surprise, to discover that Harriet had joined us. She must have jumped up onto the bed while we were chatting, and was now gazing upon the peaceful scene with a strange little smile on her furry face.

"Love?" I said. "Um, I don't think so. I think she's counting the pores on his nose. And judging from the time it's taking her there are a lot of them."

"Or the stubble on his cheeks," said Dooley. "The man has a lot of stubble."

"Exactly," I said. "Lots of stubble and lots of pores so plenty to look at."

"Oh, you silly, silly boys," said Harriet good-naturedly.

"Can't you see Odelia is in love and is simply drinking in the sheer beauty of her beloved?"

I studied the scene with this new information in mind. "Nope," I said finally. "I don't see it."

"That's because you've never been in love," said Harriet curtly.

"Oh, I've been in love," I said. "I've been in love plenty of times. But even then I didn't stare at the face of my beloved like some doofus."

"Odelia is not a doofus," said Harriet. "She's a woman in love, and that's what a woman in love looks like when faced with the object of her affection."

I studied Odelia more closely. Her lips were curved in a tiny smile, her half-lidded eyes sparkled, and a blush mantled her cheeks. All in all she looked a little dopey. As if she needed to go poo-poo and didn't want to wake up Chase.

"I think she needs to go wee-wee and she's afraid to wake him," said Dooley, proving that we were kindred spirits.

Harriet rolled her eyes in that expressive way only she can pull off.

"Ugh. You guys are so dumb," she said.

"It's obvious," said Dooley. "And I can't believe you can't see it."

"Apart from the fact that I think she needs to go poo-poo and not wee-wee, Dooley is right," I said. "This is obviously a woman who is silently praying for her boyfriend to finally wake up so she can make a run for the bathroom."

"I'm telling you it's love! How can you confuse love with having to go wee-wee or poo-poo!" Odelia uttered a little sigh, and the three of us looked up. "See?" said Harriet triumphantly. "Only a person in love can produce such a delightful little sigh."

"It's the sigh of a woman who needs to go pee-pee and knows she can't go," said Dooley, sticking to his guns.

Suddenly a deep, rumbling voice echoed through the room. "When are those darned cats going to shut up?" The voice was Chase's and obviously, in spite of our best efforts, we hadn't been as quiet and respectful as we'd hoped.

"Finally," I said. "He's awake. Now Odelia can stop counting his pores and his stubble and go to the bathroom."

"A bowl of kibble says they're going to snuggle," said Harriet. "Because snuggling is what humans in love always do."

"You're on," I said. "A bowl of kibble says she's going to take this opportunity to make a run for the bathroom."

But we were both disappointed, and the bet would have to remain a toss-up. For at that exact moment the front doorbell jangled, and both Odelia and Chase uttered a groan of annoyance and made to get up and start their day.

Unfortunately Chase did this with a little less tact and care than Odelia, and the upshot was that his sudden movements bumped Harriet from the bed and onto the carpeted floor, then also sent Dooley flying. The only one still in position was me, and I carefully watched Odelia as she swung her feet to the floor. "A bowl of kibble says Chase will go downstairs to open the door and Odelia is going to race to the bathroom," I said, still wanting to win my bet.

Three pairs of cat's eyes watched carefully as two humans stuck their feet into their respective slippers—a pair of Hello Kitty slippers for Odelia and boring old brown ones for Chase—and got up. They both moved out of the room, but before reaching the door Chase took a sharp left turn and muttered, "Can you get that, babe? I need to take a wee." And before she had the chance to respond, he'd closed the bathroom door behind him and that was that.

Talk about a shock twist! Which just goes to show that human behavior is very hard to predict indeed.

"All bets are off," said Dooley, sounding disappointed.

"And we still don't know why Odelia was staring at Chase's face for the best part of an hour," I added, equally disappointed.

"Love!" Harriet cried as she padded to the door. "I keep telling you. Love!"

"Yeah, right," I said. Only a female feline could come up with a dumb theory like that. Dooley and I exchanged a knowing glance. We were in agreement: Harriet was crazy. And we didn't even need to bet kibble over that. It was a fact, borne out by long association with the white-haired Persian.

And since we were all up now we decided to follow in Odelia's footsteps and see who this early morning visitor could be. Even before we'd set paw on the first step of the stairs, I recognized the voice of Odelia's uncle Alec, Hampton Cove's police chief and generally a harbinger of bad news.

"Uh-oh," I said. "This can't be good."

We hurried down the stairs, all questions regarding human behavior wiped from our minds. And as we arrived in the living room, the first words I heard were, "He was dead when we got there. Dead as a dodo."

I heaved a deep sigh. I may not know why humans like to stare at one another in the early morning, but here's one thing I do know: humans simply can't seem to stop murdering each other. The good thing, of course, is that this unseemly habit provides a steady flow of income for the fine upstanding men and women employed by the Hampton Cove Police Department. And Odelia.

I probably should have mentioned this before, but Odelia is by way of being a local sleuthhound. Officially she's a reporter for the *Hampton Cove Gazette*, but her natural curiosity and keen intelligence have turned her into something of a local amateur detective. And that's where the four of us come in. As cats we have access to all those places that are usually off-limits even to your intrepid reporter-slash-sleuth. Places only cats can sneak into unseen and unheard, and pick up those precious tidbits of information that are not designed for snooping eyes and ears. Plus, we get to talk to all the other cats that freely roam our town, along with its resident animal population, wild or domesticated, large or small. And it provides us what a pretty accurate picture of what goes on in our town at all times, which we then dutifully convey to Odelia, and which has helped her solve numerous crimes so far.

I know they say cats are selfish and solitary creatures, and if a human wants to choose a partner from the animal kingdom they should pick a dog. Well, that's where they would be wrong. Dogs, because of their natural tendency to shoot their mouths off and trip over their own clumsy feet, are the worst sidekick imaginable. If you really want to get the job done, you should pick a cat. Discreet, silent as the night, and naturally nosy, we are the perfect amateur sleuth's assistant, and that isn't merely my humble opinion. It's a fact.

"So who's dead?" asked Odelia, stifling a yawn.

Uncle Alec, a ruddy-faced man with russet sideburns and only a few token hairs left on top of his head, cocked an eyebrow. "Have you ever heard of Leonidas Flake?"

Odelia frowned. "The fashion designer?"

Uncle Alec nodded. "That's the one."

"He died?"

"He died," the portly police chief confirmed. "And what's more, we know exactly who did it."

"Who?"

"Gabriel Crier. His partner of thirty years. We found him with the bloody knife in his hands, bent over the corpse of his dead lover."

"If you know who did it, then why are you here?" Odelia asked.

He shrugged. "I just figured you'd like to have the scoop."

Odelia's face twisted into a wide smile. "I love you, Uncle Alec."

"I know you do. Now where the hell is Chase? I've been trying to call him all morning."

CHAPTER 2

*C*hase joined his boss and Odelia in the kitchen. Odelia had made the three of them a pot of her trademark strong coffee and they were now sipping from the tasty black brew, accompanied by toasted waffles for Uncle Alec, yogurt for Odelia, and a bowl of cereal for Chase.

"You should watch that stuff," said Odelia, pointing to the warm waffle her uncle was devouring.

Alec blinked. "Watch the waffle?" he stared at the thing as if expecting some bug to come crawling out.

"It contains a lot of bad stuff. Palm oil, for one thing. And you know what palm oil does for your cholesterol, Uncle Alec."

He stared at her. "Um, no, I don't."

"It's bad for you, all right? Just… try not to eat too much of it."

He gave her a sheepish nod, then shoved the rest of his waffle home. He'd sprayed a liberal helping of whipped cream from the can on top of it, and now licked the remnants from his fingers. There were a lot of people in Alec's life who tried to make him eat the right thing, and who had taken it upon themselves to alter his diet for the better. Only problem was, Uncle Alec was a bachelor, and what he did in the sanctity of his own home was nobody's business but his own, an opinion he stuck to diligently. Chase had lived with the big guy for a while, and seen firsthand the kind of diet the Chief kept. Many were the nights the two of them had sat on the big couch in Alec's living room, watching a game on the big TV and shoving down burgers, slices of pepperoni pizza and chips. Washed down with beer, it added to the impressive belly the police chief had managed to construct around his midsection.

Good thing, at least, that he usually ate his dinners at his sister Marge's place, who made sure her brother got some wholesome nourishment in him.

"So if this fashion designer was killed with a knife," said Odelia, "and his boyfriend was found standing over him with that same knife clutched in his hand, blood all over him, has he confessed to the crime already?"

"Funny you should ask that," said Uncle Alec. "No, he hasn't."

Odelia cut a glance to her boyfriend, who'd risen from the table and was now engaged in his favorite morning ritual of preparing a protein shake to take into the office. "So... he's claiming to be innocent or what?" asked Chase.

"Not exactly," said Alec, digging a knife into the pot of Nutella and applying an ample spread to his next waffle and ignoring Odelia's look of concern. "He has no recollection of the crime."

"What do you mean?" asked Odelia.

"He has no idea how he got there, how the knife got into his hand, and how his dead boyfriend got dead in the first place. Complete blackout."

"Who is this Gabriel Crier anyway?" asked Chase.

Alec took his little notebook from his front shirt pocket

and flipped it open. He cleared his throat noisily. "Gabriel Jake Crier. Fifty-four. Worked as a hairstylist to the stars for a while, before meeting Leonidas Flake at an art show in Paris and becoming his personal hairdresser and then something more."

"How old was Leonidas?" asked Odelia, gratefully accepting the protein shake Chase had just mixed up.

"Um, seventy-eight, and still going strong by all accounts," said Alec, kindly refusing a similar offer.

"It's good for you," Odelia pointed out. "Drink it. You'll like it. It's a vitamin bomb and you'll feel much better."

"It tastes like horse piss."

Instead of being insulted, Chase laughed loudly. "And how would you know what horse piss tastes like?"

"I don't have to taste it to know what it tastes like," said Alec, with the kind of strange logic the unhealthy use to remain unhealthy. He took a pack of cigarettes from his other front shirt pocket and shook one out.

Odelia watched on in horror. "Don't tell me you started smoking again!"

"No, I haven't," he said. "But I can't seem to shake the habit of taking one out of the pack from time to time." And as he said it, he put the cigarette to his lips. He smiled a beatific smile. "Feels so good," he muttered, then grudgingly put it away again and returned the pack to his shirt pocket. "Where were we?"

"So Gabriel Crier worked for Leonidas Flake as his personal hairstylist and something more?" Chase prompted as he licked the green sludge from his lips.

"Right. He was also rumored to be the designer's right-hand man."

"As a fashion designer?" asked Odelia.

"Was he any good?"

"Who knows," said the chief with a sigh. "I know about as

much about fashion as the next chief of police." He tucked away his little notebook.

"Maybe he felt things weren't moving along fast enough?" Odelia said. "And so he figured if he killed his boyfriend he'd become the new top guy?"

"Yeah, but that's just it. I talked to the guy's attorney early this morning. As far as he knows the most recent will and testament doesn't exactly hand the keys to the kingdom to the boyfriend. On the contrary. Everything goes to—"

"The kids?" Chase offered.

"Siblings?" Odelia guessed.

"—his cat," said Uncle Alec with a quick look towards the living room couch, where four cats sat listening to the kitchen counter conversation—Brutus had joined his friends, who had all made themselves comfortable.

"What?" asked Chase with a laugh. "A cat is inheriting the Leonidas Flake empire?"

"Looks like," said Alec. "Unless Mr. Flake made a last-minute change his attorney isn't aware of—and this seems very unlikely—the cat gets everything. The millions, the brand, the stores, the global fashion empire."

Odelia frowned. "I don't get it. How can a cat inherit a company?"

"Yeah, a cat can't run a business, can it?" said Chase, directing his question at Odelia, just to be on the safe side. She was, after all, the feline expert.

"I guess a cat could run a company," she said slowly, "if that cat knew a thing or two about business. But they would still have to relay all of the decisions through a human, who would then have to organize the actual day-to-day running of the business along those instructions. It would require a person who could intuit the cat's decision-making process, of course."

"A person like you, you mean," said Chase, who'd recently

been made aware of the fact that his fiancée was one of those rare people who could actually communicate with cats.

She nodded.

Chase turned to Alec. "And did Flake have such a person on the payroll?"

"That was Gabriel's task," he said. "He was in charge of Pussy's routine. Pussy being the name of Flake's cat. Mr. Crier took Pussy to her weekly visits to the pet salon, kept a close eye on her diet, organized her parties—"

"Sorry, her parties?" asked Chase.

"Yes, apparently this Pussy has a very busy social life, and as a rule Mr. Crier planned a lot of activities for her—she had a full schedule."

"Who told you all this stuff?" asked Odelia.

Alec dragged a meaty paw through the devastated area that was his scalp. "You'd be surprised how chatty staff members of the recently departed can be."

"You should have called," said Chase. "I would have helped set up the interviews."

"I did call you," said Uncle Alec. "And Odelia."

Both Odelia and Chase grabbed for their phones. "Shoot," Chase muttered. "Must have forgotten to plug the darn thing in last night."

"Same here," said Odelia, taking Chase's phone and proceeding to plug in both phones so they could recharge before they left the house.

"Anyway, it's a slam-dunk case," said Alec, eagerly checking out the uneaten waffle on his niece's plate and gratefully accepting it when she handed it to him. "Crier was caught red-handed, so I'm guessing we'll be done with this before lunch. Still, always good to cross our T's and dot our I's."

"Weird that the only person who stands to gain from the

designer's death is the man's cat," said Chase. "What do you make of that, Chief?"

He lowered his bristly brows into a frown. "Not sure, buddy. But you have to allow for the fact that these are celebrities, and as we all know celebrities are eccentric. Leonidas only changed his will last week. The one before that had the boyfriend as the main beneficiary, so there's always a chance he didn't know Flake cut him out of his will."

"I think the cat did it," Chase quipped.

"Funny guy," the Chief grumbled.

Odelia glanced over to her cats, who were listening attentively. "Did you hear that, you guys? Looks like we have a feline suspect for this one."

"Impossible," said Max. "A cat would never kill a human."

"I'm not so sure," said Brutus. "If that human treated him or her badly, anything is possible."

"But he was stabbed with a knife," Max pointed out. "Cats don't stab people with knives, Brutus."

"Cats don't need knives," said Harriet. "We use our inbuilt tools." And she unsheathed a razor-sharp claw to turn her words into a show-and-tell.

"Was he stabbed with the knife Crier was holding?" asked Odelia now.

"Um... not sure," said Alec. "Abe is delayed." He checked his watch. "He should be there shortly, though, so I better start heading back over there."

Odelia jumped down from the kitchen stool. "You mean to say the body is still there? The coroner hasn't even examined the victim?"

"Nope," said Alec with faux cheer. "Which is why I figured I might as well pick up you two, so you can give me a hand wrapping this thing up."

"We better get going," said Odelia. "I can't believe we've been sitting here chatting while that poor man is lying there."

"He's not going anywhere," said Alec, buttering a piece of toast.

"And I haven't taken a shower yet," said Odelia, patting her hair.

"You look fine," said Chase.

"Oh, God," she muttered. She hated leaving the house without taking a shower or putting on a fresh set of threads. "Give me five minutes."

"You can take ten," said Uncle Alec, unconcerned.

She hurried up the stairs, and took the quickest shower in the history of mankind, put on a pair of jeans, pulled a T-shirt and sweater over her head, and decided to forgo drying her hair for once, then hurried down again.

Alec and Chase were still chatting away, not a care in the world.

"Cats don't frame humans," Uncle Alec was saying. "That's a fact. I mean, no offense to you guys," he added, gesturing to Max and the others, "but I don't think you have it in you to try and frame someone for a crime you committed. Am I right or am I right?"

"Cats may be a lot of things but we're not that cunning," Brutus agreed.

"I wouldn't be too sure about that," said Harriet. "Cats can be very, very cunning."

"What is he saying, honey?" asked Alec.

"He's saying cats are not that cunning," said Odelia, shoving her notebook into her purse and checking the kitchen to see if all the appliances were turned off.

"And then there's the logistics of the thing," said Chase. "How would a cat kill a person, then plant the knife into the hand of another person, without that person's knowledge? It can't be done. No, I think you're right, Alec. The case is open-and-shut. All we need to do is get a confession and we're done."

"That's the plan," said Alec. He got down from the kitchen stool and hoisted up his pants. "Well, let's get going, kids. Chateau Leonidas awaits us."

"Chateau Leonidas?" asked Chase. "Why am I not surprised that the man lived in an actual castle?"

"Because if you're one of the most successful designers in the world, of course you live in a castle," said Alec. "Besides, he's French, so there's that."

"Do all French people live in castles?" asked Dooley.

"No, I don't think they do, Dooley," said Odelia with a smile. "Only the very wealthy."

"Oh," said Dooley, looking slightly disappointed.

"I, for one, can't wait to meet this Pussy," said Brutus with relish, then, when he caught Harriet's sideways glance, quickly added, "I mean, so we can talk to her, and find out what she knows."

Harriet, who'd narrowed her eyes, didn't seem all that excited at the prospect of meeting what could very well be the richest cat in the world. And as she extended and retracted her claws a few times, Odelia thought she could actually see Brutus's Adam's apple nervously shift up and down.

She hadn't even known cats actually had an Adam's apple.

CHAPTER 3

I glanced over to my feline comrades. It's one thing to act as a sleuthcat, but another to have to investigate a fellow cat for a crime they may or may not have committed. At least for me this marked the first occasion that a cat had been singled out as a possible suspect in a heinous crime like murder. Usually cats, when accused of a crime, are only guilty of misdemeanors like destroying a beloved set of curtains, a nice carpet here or there or stealing a fish from the fishmonger's slab. I've even known a cat who chased little chicks around the backyard of some minor amateur chicken farmer. When interviewed after the fact, he claimed to have been looking for a feathered little friend to play with.

"Cats can be killers, though," said Harriet seriously. "Cats have been known to kill birds and mice and on occasion even a rat or two."

"Cats kill fish," said Dooley, adding his two cents to the discussion.

"Don't talk nonsense," said Brutus brusquely. "Cats don't kill fish."

"They do!" said Dooley. "I once saw Shadow racing down Main Street with a complete fish between his teeth."

"I'm sure Shadow didn't catch that fish," said Harriet.

"No, he did," Dooley insisted. "He got it from Wilbur Vickery's store."

We all laughed, except for Dooley, who didn't seem to get the joke.

"That fish was already dead, Dooley," I said finally, when he merely stared at me, clearly expecting me to provide him with an explanation for the sudden chucklefest.

"Dead? I don't think so."

"Fish live in the sea," I said, "or in rivers or lakes or even the occasional pond. They don't hang around Wilbur Vickery's General Store."

"The fish Vickery sells is caught by fishermen," Harriet said. "Men who fish. In the sea," she added, as if addressing a not-so-clever kitten.

"Oh," said Dooley, clearly disappointed that his war story turned out to be a benign little tale instead. "Well, he did catch it, even if it was dead already."

"Just like I catch my kibble every day," Brutus said with a grin.

Harriet clapped her paws. "Order, people. Let's come to order," she said. "Let's focus on the task at hand. We won't be able to help Odelia by telling tall tales of Shadow stealing fish from the General Store. We need to decide once and for all if cats are capable of homicide—in other words, the killing of a hominid."

"A what?" asked Brutus.

"A hominid. A member of the family of the Hominidae or great apes."

"A human," I explained.

"Oh, right," said Brutus.

"I once saw a story about a cat that likes to lie on top of its human's face," said Dooley. When we all stared at him, he added, "It was on the Discovery Channel so it must be true!"

"So did the human die?" asked Harriet.

"Yeah, that's the real issue here," Brutus added. "Did that human die?"

"I don't think so," said Dooley, frowning as he searched his memory. "No, I think he survived. At least he was alive when they interviewed him."

More eye rolls greeted Dooley's second contribution to our discussion, with some exasperated groans coming from Harriet, but once again it was up to me to explain to my dear friend what the problem was with his story.

"Dooley, if they interviewed the man after the fact, and he was able to recount the experience, he didn't die, see?"

He thought about this for a moment, then conceded, "No, I guess he didn't."

"Why did he lie on top of his human's face?" I asked, for the story did possess an element of intrigue.

"Yeah, did he try to kill him?" asked Brutus, who has a penchant for all things violent.

"No, I think he just wanted to show his affection," said Dooley. "Or maybe he was afraid his human's face would get cold during the night."

"Well, he shouldn't have," Harriet snapped. "Lying on top of a hominid's face might block certain aspects of the breathing apparatus and kill it dead."

"What's all this talk about hominids?" I asked.

"Marge loaned me an eBook she got from the library the other day," said Harriet. "Very interesting stuff. About the different species that make up this great big beautiful planet of ours. She felt I'd been spending too much time watching the Kardashians with Gran, and I should read something that would feed my mind instead. I like it. I might read a few more of them."

I was greatly surprised, but also greatly impressed. Harriet is not exactly known as the intellectual of our gang of four, and this was all to the good.

"Look, all this talk about killer cats is all well and good," said Brutus, "but frankly I don't buy it. Not for one second."

"What don't you buy?" asked Dooley, interested.

"That cats are capable of killing humans! It's simply not possible. I mean, they can claw their humans, when provoked, or even bite them, but kill them? I don't think any member of the feline species, in the long history we share with the human race, has ever been responsible for the death of a human."

"A cat could kill if it accidentally kicked over a candle and set the house on fire," Harriet pointed out.

"Yeah, but that's not exactly murder, is it? That's more like an accident."

"Brutus is right," I said. "What we need to ask ourselves is this: are cats capable of possessing the intent to kill? Willfully murder a human being?"

We all chewed on that one for a moment, then Dooley finally said, "Do you think Pussy is one of those cats that likes to wear booties?"

"Dooley, let's try to focus on the issue at hand for a moment, shall we?" I said. "In a show of paws, who thinks cats are capable of manslaughter?"

No paws were raised. "Well, that settles it," said Harriet. "Pussy is innocent, and whoever claims she did what they say she did is lying through their teeth."

"We'll know more after we've talked to her," I said.

Odelia, who'd been surfing the internet, preparatory to launching her investigation, now called out, "Did you know that Leonidas was couturier to kings and queens and presidents?"

"No, I did not know that," I said, but when Chase joined

her at the computer it dawned on me that her question hadn't actually been directed at me.

Instead, Chase said, "Well what do you know?"

I stared at my human for a moment, then back at my posse. They quickly looked away. It had been an embarrassing moment for me, and none of them wanted to rub my face in it. Which was nice of them, I guess. Then again, it highlighted a growing concern we all shared: ever since Chase had moved in, our face time with Odelia had gradually diminished to the point it had almost been reduced to zero. Used to be she spent all of her free time with us, or her family, who live right next door. These days she spends most of her time with Chase, and what little time is left, she devotes to taking care of our basic needs. It's been an adjustment, let me tell you, and one we're struggling with.

"It's all right, Maxie, baby," said Brutus finally. "It's happened to us all."

And it had, which meant it was turning into a serious problem. I mean, what good is it to be able to talk to your human, if that human is always busy talking to her significant other human? None whatsoever, right?

Anyway, I know I'm nagging and whining, which is so not me. Cats rarely nag and whine. At least not this cat. Still, being ignored by your favorite human in all the world is a tough one, and if I hadn't known better I'd have thought Odelia sometimes did it on purpose, to show us that things had changed around here. That we were no longer her top priority.

Just then Odelia and Chase moved to the door, then passed out into the street and we could hear the key being turned in the lock. Silence reigned for a moment, as we all stared at the closed door. Finally, Harriet spoke. "Correct me if I'm wrong, you guys. But did Odelia just forget to take us along?"

CHAPTER 4

*O*delia was already in her pickup and maneuvering the vehicle away from the curb when she felt Chase's eyes raking her visage.

"What?" she asked as she reached the end of the road, then flashed her blinker to take the turn.

"Aren't you forgetting something?" asked Chase, looking amused.

"Forget what?" she asked, her mind now occupied by all that she'd read on Leonidas Flake. The man had lived a full life, that much was obvious. Born in Paris, France, he'd launched himself as a contender in the fashion trade in the sixties. He'd worked for several of the big fashion houses before establishing his own brand, which had made him a household name over the course of the six decades he'd been in the business. Now everyone the world over, from the cognoscenti to the non-cognoscenti, was aware of the name Leonidas Flake. A name that brought to mind gorgeous haute couture, but also couture designed for the masses, in his prêt-à-porter collections and collaborations with some of the major clothing retailers like Gap, Banana Republic, J. Crew and H&M.

"Weren't you planning on taking your cats along?" asked Chase now.

She frowned at him, then glanced over her shoulder. "Oh, God," she said, suddenly mortified. "I forgot my cats!"

"That's what I figured."

Immediately she performed a U-turn and before long was right back where she started. She cut the engine but before she could jump from the vehicle, Chase had already beaten her to the punch.

"I'll get them," he said.

She shook her head in dismay. What was wrong with her? She'd never ever forgotten her cats before. Never. Her excuse, of course, was that she'd been so busy thinking about the case her uncle had landed in her lap that she'd totally forgotten about her little dears. As she glanced over, she saw them walking out of the house, single file, right behind Chase. They didn't look happy. In fact Max was giving her an accusatory look that she absolutely deserved.

They hopped into the car without a word, then sat silently staring before them, not deigning her a single glance.

"Look, I'm sorry, all right?" she tried. "I was so wrapped up in this Leonidas business that I completely forgot. I'm so, so sorry, you guys."

"We can forgive you, Odelia," finally spoke Harriet, "but we'll never forget."

Her words elicited a snicker from Brutus, but the nasty glance she gave him quickly shut him up.

"What do you mean?" Odelia asked.

"It means we're insulted," said Harriet. "And a cat never forgets."

"I think that's elephants, though," said Max.

"Cats, too," said Dooley. "We have a mind like a steel trap."

"That's elephants," Max insisted. "Elephants never forget a face, or if someone stepped on their toe at some point. They will take revenge, even if years have passed since the toe-stepping incident."

"How can someone step on an elephant's toes?" said Brutus. "Have you seen an elephant's foot? He doesn't even have toes."

"An elephant does have toes," Max insisted stubbornly, "and if you step on them he'll never forget your face, and the first chance he gets, even if a hundred years have passed, he'll step right back on your toes. Quid pro quo."

"Quit what?" asked Brutus.

"If an elephant stepped on my toes I'd be flat as a pancake," said Harriet.

"I'm sure it's not elephants but cats that never forget a face," said Dooley. "It was on the Discovery Channel."

"Oh, my God!" said Harriet. "Will you shut up about the Discovery Channel for one minute!"

Odelia turned back to face the front, put the car in gear, and soon they were tootling along the road in perfect silence, apart from Dooley's occasional mutterings about elephants and things he'd seen on the Discovery Channel.

They made good time, and before long had left Hampton Cove behind and were driving along the coast, where all the billionaires lived—and the occasional millionaire who got lost when looking to land a house deal. This was celebrity land, with more celebrities living in close proximity than in probably any other place in the country, except, of course, Beverly Hills or Malibu, where celebrities tend to spring up like a rash, or a fungoid growth.

"Nice houses," said Chase finally as they passed million-dollar home after million-dollar home. Not that there was a lot to see, as billionaires are notoriously shy, and don't like to show their faces or even their million-dollar dwellings, except in the form of an exclusive spread in *Architectural Digest*.

"I wouldn't mind living here," said Harriet as she stared out the window.

"I would," said Max, surprisingly. "I like my home just the way it is."

"Small, you mean?" asked Harriet.

"Cozy," he countered. "These McMansions are so gigantic you can spend days wandering around without meeting a single soul. You could probably get lost and only be found when there's nothing left of you but a rotting carcass."

"Aren't we in a sunny mood?" said Brutus.

"Just a passing thought," said Max.

"You exaggerate, Max," said Harriet, who liked her celebrities.

"No, I don't. And it's probably the reason these celebrity couples never stick it out for more than a couple of months. They move in together, then never see each other again as they live in separate wings, and if they do happen to run into each other they haven't seen each other for so long they don't even recognize their spouse and call the police to report a prowler."

The cats all laughed at this, and so did Odelia. The only one who didn't laugh was Chase, which was understandable, as he didn't understand the finer points of the feline language. So Odelia translated the joke to him and he nodded. "I think there's a lot of wisdom in that," he said. "Who said it? Max?"

"Hey," said Brutus. "Why does it always have to be Max who says the clever stuff? I'm clever, too!"

"It was Brutus," said Odelia quickly, in an attempt to pour oil on trouble waters.

"No, it wasn't," Brutus muttered.

"Oh?" said Chase, sounding surprised.

"Why is he sounding so surprised?" asked Brutus. "I'm a very clever cat!"

"Don't act so surprised," said Odelia. "Brutus feels a little offended."

"I'm right here!" said Brutus.

"Well, I didn't mean to," said Chase. "It's just that you mention Max the most, and hardly ever talk about the others."

Odelia felt heat rise to her cheeks. "Chase," she said. "Maybe you shouldn't…"

"Shouldn't what?" said Harriet, whose eyes had turned into tiny slits. "Mention that Max is your favorite? Oh, but we've known about that for a long time, haven't we?"

"Yes, we have," Brutus grumbled.

"You guys, I'm not Odelia's favorite," said Max, laughing. "Not by a mile. In fact if there's one favorite in Odelia's life it's Chase."

"Max is right," said Dooley. "He used to be the favorite but now Chase is."

"You guys!" said Odelia, mortified. "How many times do I have to tell you? I don't play favorites! I love you all the same."

"Is that why you hardly ever spend time with us anymore?" asked Harriet now. "And why you spend all of your time with Chase?"

"Look, if I have, I'm sorry, all right?" Had she been spending all of her time with Chase? Hard to imagine. Then again, maybe Harriet was right. Since Chase had moved in they had been spending a lot of time together. And lately they'd gone on a lot of dates—movie nights, dinners, the odd show or concert.

"Look, if I have neglected you, I promise I'll make it up to you, all right?"

"And how are you going to do that?" asked Harriet, who

seemed to be the self-appointed president of the cat complaints committee.

"I'll… take you all out on a date. Just the five of us. We'll hang out all night and have the time of our lives."

"We're cats, Odelia," said Max. "We don't go out on dates."

"Yeah, you're confusing us with dogs," said Harriet.

"So what would you like to do?" she asked, desperate to make it up to her feline menagerie.

"Just spend a cozy evening at home," said Max.

"Without Chase, you mean?"

Max hesitated, then stuck his head together with the others while they seriously considered this question.

Finally, they broke the huddle and Max cleared his throat. "We don't mind if Chase is there, as long as we all get snuggle time on the couch with you."

"We'll time it," Dooley suggested. "There's five of us, Chase included, so you can spend fifty percent of your time paying attention to us, and fifty percent to Chase."

"I don't think that's fair," said Brutus. "We should all get twelve percent of her time. Fair is fair."

"What are those precious little furballs talking about?" asked Chase with a smile. He still found it hilarious that Odelia's cats could talk.

"We're in the middle of a negotiation. One night spent at home, with equal face time with me. Right now we're at twelve percent for each of you."

"Huh. Interesting."

"One night isn't enough," said Max. "I'd say you spend one night out on the town with Chase, the other nights at home with us. Take it or leave it."

"You drive a hard bargain, Max," she said.

"Strictly speaking she should spend 1.4 nights with Chase, and 5.6 nights with us," said Dooley, who'd clearly been making complicated calculations in his head.

"We can work out the details later," said Harriet. "Right now all we want from you is a preliminary agreement."

"Um…" said Odelia. She'd suddenly noticed that a car had been following them for a while now. It wasn't trying very hard not to be noticed either: the little red Peugeot was almost bumper to bumper with Odelia's pickup, and the little old lady that sat behind the wheel had her face practically plastered to the windshield and was staring at them intently.

Chase had noticed, too, for he suddenly asked, a slight note of worry in his voice, "Um, babe? Why is your grandmother trying to ram us off the road?"

CHAPTER 5

*I*f there's one thing I'm grateful for it is that cats are not able to drive cars. The plain truth of the matter is that I don't like cars. What's to like, really? Cars smell funny, they're cramped and closed off, like a big metal box, and they move way too fast most of the time. And then of course there's the fact that cats don't wear seatbelts. I mean, the first car manufacturer who designs seatbelts for pets still has to arrive on the scene. Elon Musk, maybe? At any rate, even if seatbelts for pets were invented, I don't think I'd use them. Too confining. They'd probably feel like a noose, or, worse, a leash, and as you well know cats don't condone leashes. We're not dogs, for crying out loud!

One of the issues that vex me when riding in cars with strangers, or even non-strangers like Odelia, is the harrowing driving style of most humans. They drive their cars as if they're bumper cars, looking for other cars they can hit. Humans seem to enjoy driving at breakneck speeds through places teeming with people, pets and kids, where at any given moment one of those people, pets or kids might wander into the flight path of the incoming vehicle and be run over. It's one of those absurdities I've never understood. One of those maniacs was now giving chase, flashing their lights and leaning on their horn, probably wanting to overtake us but not being able to, due to space constraints on this stretch of road, as well as cars coming from the opposite direction. Then, when I glanced back, to see who this road rage person could be, I was surprised to find that it was none other than Grandma Muffin!

Then again, I probably shouldn't have been too surprised. Gran is the worst driver known to man, and that is saying something. She drives as if she's the only person on the road, which was probably the case back when she got her license, but in the meantime more drivers have arrived on the scene, a fact which irks her to such an extent she tries to remove them from her path like corn before her sickle. She usually drives Marge's little red Peugeot, since Marge doesn't really need it to go to work, the library being within walking distance from the house. If I were Uncle Alec, though, I'd have grounded Gran a long time ago. A question of protecting the safety of the many from the lack of driving skills of the few, if you see what I mean.

"I think she wants us to pull over," said Odelia now.

"I think she wants to *run* us over," said Chase, craning his neck.

Odelia slowed down the car, then parked it on the shoulder. Grandma, true to Chase's predictions, pulled over right behind us and got out. She didn't look happy. In fact it wasn't too much to say she looked livid.

"Hey!" she shouted even before she'd reached us. "Hey, you!"

Odelia rolled down the window. "Gran. What's wrong?"

"I had to hear it from Tex, who had to hear it from Marge, who had to hear it from Alec!" she said, shaking her fists like one about to blow her top.

"Hear what?" asked Odelia.

"That there's been a murder!"

"Has there been a murder?" asked Odelia.

"Don't you play dumb with me, missy!" said Gran, still fuming.

Grandma Muffin, who is Marge and Alec's mother, is a little old lady, with tiny white curls and tiny round glasses. She looks like Sylvester Stallone's mom in that ageless classic *Stop! Or My Mom Will Shoot* if Estelle Getty hadn't dyed her hair in that one. If you see Gran for the first time you might be mistaken to think she's one of those sweet old ladies who bake cookies for her grandkids and read them bed-time stories. Gran isn't like that. She's more likely to shoot you where you stand than sing a lullaby. At least if New York gun laws weren't so strict, and if her son didn't keep a close eye on her.

"So why wasn't I invited?" she demanded, practically stomping her foot.

"Invited to what?" asked Odelia, still playing coy.

"To the murder! You know how much I like a good murder!"

"Nobody likes a murder, Gran," said Odelia. "Murders are horrible, and not something to be enjoyed."

"You promised me I could tag along when you had another murder case. You know as well as I do what a great team we make. Like Starsky and Hutch. I'm Hutch, of course, the pretty one, and you're the Brooklyn babe."

"I'm not from Brooklyn."

"Who cares! We're a team! You don't break up the team!"

Odelia rubbed her eyes. "Well, I guess I didn't want to wake you."

"Wake me! I've been up since five! I was up while you were still in la la land!" She stuck her head in the window and directed a scathing look at Chase. "You!"

"Ma'am?" said Chase, meeting Gran's kindling eye.

She wagged a bony finger at him. "You should be ashamed of yourself, Detective Kingsley. Hogging my granddaughter's time like that. You know as well as I do that I only got a couple of good years left to spend with my one and only grandchild, and you're stealing it!"

"I'm very sorry, ma'am," he said, trying not to grin and failing.

"What's with all the ma'am crap! It's Mrs. Muffin!"

"Of course, Mrs. Muffin."

"I could be dead tomorrow, and because of you Odelia would have missed her last chance to spend some quality time with her favorite granny."

"You're my only granny, Gran," said Odelia.

"Only because Tex's folks were a bunch of ninnies who croaked before their time. It just goes to show we should cherish the little time we have."

"Hop in, Mrs. Muffin," said Chase. "We were just driving down to check out the murder scene now."

"I'm not hopping in with you. Not after having been so rudely ignored. But I will drive along behind you. Who's in charge of this here investigation?"

"I guess I am," said Chase, as if the thought had only now occurred to him.

"Consider me your sidekick from now on. I'm sticking to you like glue!"

And with these words full of promise, she stomped back to her vehicle, got in and slammed the door, then sat staring at us with an expectant look.

"We better do as she says," said Chase. "I have a feeling she'll kill us if we don't."

"I'd really hoped she'd sit this one out," said Odelia as she started the car.

"Oh, so you *did* leave her behind on purpose."

She shrugged. "I didn't think it through."

"Great," he said. "And now she'll stick to me like glue." But he was grinning, indicating he didn't mind.

"Amazing," said Harriet quietly, as Odelia and Chase discussed the logistics of running an investigation consisting of one police detective, one local reporter, and one little old lady with no clear designation or authority.

"What is?" I asked.

"Haven't you been listening? First Odelia leaves us behind, and then she purposely decides to ditch Gran. Don't you see what's going on here?"

I had a feeling I was going to find out soon, whether I replied in the affirmative or not.

"She's engaged to be married now, and slowly but surely she's edging us all out! Her cats, her grandmother—all of us!"

"No, she's not," I said automatically, for I rarely believe anything negative about my human.

"Yes, she is! Once she's married she's going to get rid of us, and then she's going to get rid of Gran, too!"

"But why would she do that? She loves us," said Dooley. "And she loves her grandmother, too. Doesn't she?"

"No, she doesn't," said Harriet. She groaned. "I can't believe I've been so stupid! Don't you see? She's been wanting to get rid of us all along, and now she's found the perfect excuse."

"The wedding?" asked Brutus.

"Yes! The wedding! She'll get married, and that will be the end of this." She was gesturing vaguely between us and Odelia.

We all stared dumbly at her paw motions.

"What's… this?" I asked, mimicking the gesture.

"The bond we share! This rare and unique fellowship of cats and humans. Clearly she's sick and tired of having to lug us all over the place like so much ballast, and her grandmother, too. Didn't you catch the dirty looks she gave poor Gran? She can't wait to be rid of her, and us. Free at last!"

We stared at her, the harbinger of such terrible and upsetting news.

"I think Harriet is right," said Brutus. "Odelia is getting ready to dump us."

"But what is she going to do with us?" asked Dooley, sounding panicky.

I should probably point out that it doesn't take much for Dooley to panic. And being abandoned by our dear, sweet human definitely fit the bill.

"She'll probably try to dump us on Marge and Tex," said Harriet. "And then she and Chase are finally free to live their lives unencumbered by the presence of four cats and an annoying old grandmother."

Her words had a chilling effect on us, and the rest of the drive we were all conspicuously silent. And as I turned Harriet's words over in my mind, I had to admit they made sense. Odelia had been spending less and less time with us, giving us less and less attention, and this morning she'd even 'forgotten' to bring us along, just as she'd 'forgotten' about Gran, who loved to go on these little outings with her granddaughter.

Could it be that she and Chase had a secret plan? That they were getting ready to move away from Hampton Cove, maybe even overseas? They'd clearly had a ball in England, and since Odelia was a reporter she could very easily get a job anywhere, and Chase being a cop he could have already landed himself a snazzy position in Europol or Interpol or some other pol. My heart sank as I contemplated this terrible prospect. We'd still be taken care of, of course, and Marge and Tex and Gran were wonderful people. Only problem was: they weren't my people, per se. I only had one people and that was Odelia, and the prospect of never seeing her again suddenly filled me with dread.

And so it was with a sinking heart that I watched Odelia expertly navigate the car in the direction of a tall iron gate, which swung open the moment we arrived, then swung closed again behind Gran's little red car.

Suddenly I didn't feel like cracking this case.

Because it could very well be our last one.

CHAPTER 6

$\mathcal{T}$he sun shone brightly, reflecting off the abundance of glass the late Leonidas Flake had opted for when he'd commissioned an architect to build his chateau. It wasn't so much a chateau, though, but more of a bunker the designer had built. The entire structure appeared to have been constructed out of slabs of black concrete, interspersed with plate-glass windows. All in all it reminded Odelia of a gigantic Lego house, if those Legos had been used by a child who preferred his or her Legos black and slightly ominous-looking.

"It looks... a little scary," she now confessed to her partner in crime.

"It looks like a black cube," Chase said. The cop rarely minced words.

"Yeah. I don't know. I guess I expected something more along the lines of the castle of Versailles," she said as she opened the rear door of the car and allowed four cats to pour out gracefully to the gravel drive.

She crouched down, to provide them with her customary pep talk and instructions for the assignment ahead. Her loyal

37

troupe, however, instead of eagerly listening to their master's voice, as they usually did, simply ignored her and tripped off in the direction of the house.

"Huh," she said, straightening and ignoring the tiny crick in her knees. "What's gotten into them?"

But she didn't have time to contemplate the state of mind her cats were in, for Gran had parked her car right next to Odelia's and now came clambering out with some effort.

"So what's the lowdown?" the old lady asked, directing her question at Chase and ignoring her one and only grandchild.

"Victim is Leonidas Flake," said Chase. "Fashion designer of French origin. Seventy-eight years old."

"So sad when they're struck down in their prime," said Gran, clucking her tongue.

Chase frowned, then continued to give her 'the lowdown.' "Plenty of staff on the premises. Housekeeper, cleaners, chauffeur, gardener, chef... and one boyfriend, Gabriel Crier, who was discovered standing over the body, a bloodied knife in his hands."

"Who saw him?"

"One of the maids. She usually came to open the curtains in the morning, always around the same time, only this morning she found that the master was beyond waking."

"Clever," said Gran, giving Chase an encouraging pat on the back. "Keep this up and you'll go far, Detective Kingsley. Now take me to the body. I need to get a sense of the crime scene."

And without waiting for a reply, she hoofed it in the direction of the black block of concrete that was the famous designer's Hamptons home.

Chase stared after her, then scratched his scalp. "Is she now in charge of this investigation or what?"

"It would appear so," Odelia confirmed.

"And to think that there was once a time I felt very strongly about civilians poking their noses into my investigations," he said as they set foot for the house in Gran's wake.

"I remember," said Odelia with a smile. "When you first arrived in town you used to give me hell, remember?"

"Oh, I do remember," he said. "It took me a while to get used to the way things are done around here."

"You never thought you'd be running your investigations alongside a little old lady, a nosy reporter and four cats, did you?" she teased.

He chuckled lightly. "Not in a million years. Back when I was still with the NYPD I was known to be a stickler for protocol."

"Protocol will only get you so far."

"I had to learn that the hard way."

They'd reached the house and watched as Gran pressed her finger on the bell then kept on pressing it, almost drilling the thing into the wall. Inside, a distinct and very annoying buzzing sound could be heard, and the longer Gran kept pressure on the button, the louder and more annoying it became.

Finally, the door was yanked open by a breathless young woman dressed in a maid's uniform.

"Yes?" she asked, looking flustered.

"Chase Kingsley, ma'am," said Chase, producing his police badge and holding it up for her inspection. "Hampton Cove PD. And this is Odelia Poole, civilian consultant, and..." He directed a quizzical look at Gran.

"I'm Vesta Muffin," croaked Gran. "Now take me to the body!"

The woman nodded nervously, then stepped aside to admit the small band of three into the house.

"Chief Alec told me you were coming," she said. "He also

told me the coroner would be here shortly, but we haven't had the pleasure of his company yet."

"So who's been guarding the body?" asked Chase, putting his detective's cap on.

"Two of your people," said the girl. "They've been standing watch in the room where…" She gulped. "Where he was found," she finished with a sob. She took a tissue out of her pocket and pressed it to her nose. "This is all so horrible. One moment he was alive and well and the next… I mean, who would have thought he was capable?"

"Mr. Crier, you mean?" asked Chase.

The girl nodded. "Such a nice man."

"The world is a dangerous place, miss," said Gran. "You just truck along, happy as pie, and then suddenly, BOOM! Out of the blue disaster strikes. Now take me to the body, will you? I need to get a feel for the scene, and the stiff."

"Of course," said the girl, nodding. She then led the way into the house, which was as starkly modern on the inside as on the outside. There was only one color scheme, really: black and white, with shades of gray. No decorations. Black concrete walls. Gray concrete floors and ceilings. And tiny little pinpricks of halogen casting a hard light across the starkly empty rooms.

"Nice place you got here," said Gran, by way of small talk, but the maid was obviously too distraught to engage in social niceties.

"Were you the one who found Mr. Flake?" asked Odelia.

She nodded. "Yes, I was. Mr. Flake hated alarm clocks, or any indicators of time, really. He didn't wear a watch, or condone clocks in the house. We even had to get rid of the digital clock on the microwave. So he instructed me to wake him up in the morning by entering his room, and switching on the light therapy lamps. They mimic natural sunlight, you see."

"Couldn't you simply open the curtains?" asked Gran.

"Mr. Flake hated the sun. He rarely left the house."

"Like a vampire," Gran muttered.

They'd arrived at a floor-to-ceiling set of double rusty decorative sheet metal doors, and the girl halted. "I-I went in to wake him, as I usually did, at seven o'clock, only the moment I set foot inside the room, I-I saw him."

"Gabriel?" asked Odelia gently.

The girl nodded, then pressed the tissue to her nose again and closed her eyes as she relived that horrible moment.

"He was just standing there, frozen like a statue. At first I didn't know what was going on. It was dark, of course. So I cheerfully asked, 'Oh, I didn't know you were up already, sir.' He didn't respond, though, and just stood there. So I switched on the lights, and as they slowly lit up the room, that's when I saw it: he was holding a knife in his right hand, blood dripping to the floor. And he had the weirdest expression on his face."

"What expression?" asked Gran.

She shook her head, a frown on her face. "Confusion? Yes, that's probably what it was. He looked confused, and scared, and then he spoke those horrible words. 'Is he dead?' And that's when I saw Mr. Flake. His silk pajamas were streaked with blood, and his eyes were wide open, staring up into space." She shivered. "That's when I knew Mr. Crier was right. Mr. Flake was dead, and he'd killed him."

She opened the door, almost as an afterthought, and the first sight that met Odelia's eyes was the red-haired female cop standing just inside the door. She recognized her as Sarah Flunk, Chase's colleague. Sarah tipped an imaginary peaked cap to the newcomers. "Detective," she said. "Odelia." She hesitated as she fastened her eyes on Gran, then nodded in greeting. "Mrs. Muffin."

Tough to deny the mother of your boss admission to a crime scene.

Near the window, a burly cop had been stationed. His name was Randal Skip, and judging from his dark scowl he was not a man to be trifled with. When he saw Odelia, though, his crusty features crumbled into a smile. He'd always been a big fan of the boss's niece. He held up a hand in greeting.

On the bed, as the maid had found him, lay one of the most famous fashion designers of his generation. His trademark white mane was unruffled, his square face with the thin lips chalk-white as usual, and the only thing that gave away that he was dead was the fact that he wasn't breathing.

After uttering a distraught little yelp of distress, the maid fled from the room, and Sarah Flunk closed the heavy steel doors behind her.

"No one's been in or out?" asked Gran, as she took out a pair of plastic gloves from her pocket and directed an earnest look at the dead man.

"No one, ma'am," said Officer Randal Skip. "Your son told us he'd send in a team, so…" He directed a quizzical look at Chase, but the latter merely shook his head, and Randal rearranged his features into a stoic expression.

"So where's the culprit?" asked Gran now.

"You mean the boyfriend?" asked Sarah. "At the station, ma'am. Chief Alec took him into custody."

"So did he confess?"

"Not to my knowledge. But then he doesn't have to confess, does he? He was caught red-handed, so to speak."

"He was covered with his victim's blood," said Randal. "As clear-cut a case as there ever was, ma'am."

"Mh," said Gran, not convinced. "Too clear-cut, wouldn't you say?"

"Ma'am?"

"A case as clear-cut as this is a rarity. In all my years I don't think I've ever handled a case where the killer, instead of fleeing the scene of the crime, simply chose to wait for a witness to show up, if you see what I mean."

Randal cut another glance to Chase, who, once again, shook his head. 'Humor the lady,' his demeanor appeared to indicate.

"So you don't think he did it?" asked Sarah, not hiding her skepticism.

"I'm not saying he did, and I'm not saying he didn't," Gran said as she checked the body. "He looks pretty dead to me," she concluded after a long moment, then bent over to put her ear against the man's lips. Straightening, she added, "Yep, I think he's dead. What did Abe Cornwall say?"

"Hasn't shown up yet, ma'am."

"Mh," she said, then studied the wound more closely. "Stab wound would you say, Randal?"

"That would be my conclusion, ma'am," said the burly cop. "Of course I'm not an expert, but seeing as the killer was still holding the knife, that would be my best guess."

"Straight to the heart," Sarah murmured as she looked on reverently.

"A-ha," said Gran. "Of course. *Crime passionnel.*"

"I wouldn't know, ma'am. I'm not a detective."

Gran turned to Chase. "What do you say, Detective Kingsley?"

Chase had taken up position on the other side of the bed. "Any cameras?" he asked, glancing around.

"As a matter of fact there are," said Randal. He pointed to the only painting in the room. It depicted the dead man, seated on what looked like a throne, his trademark dark glasses obscuring the upper strata of his face, a white cat perched on his knee. It reminded Odelia of Dr. No, the James Bond villain.

"There's a camera embedded in the painting," Sarah explained. "It's the cat's eyes. They're actually two lenses. But we haven't been able to locate the footage."

"Did you check with Flake's security team?" asked Odelia.

"We did. The guy in charge of security reckons that either the camera is a dud—just for show—or else it fed into a parallel security system only accessible to Flake himself. At any rate he doesn't seem to have a clue."

"It must feed into something," said Gran, as she climbed on top of the bed to take a closer look at the camera. "Clever," she said. "Very clever indeed."

"There's a rumor going around that Flake and Crier used it to create their own private home movies, sir," said Sarah, addressing Chase. She lowered her voice. "Home sex movies, sir. Only we haven't been able to find them yet."

"When I talk to Crier I'll ask him about it," said Chase as he cast a worried glance at Gran, who was still trudging around on the bed, potentially disturbing the crime scene. Finally she was satisfied and climbed down.

"Kinky," she commented, then swung round with the air of one who has come to a conclusion. "Sex game gone wrong is my conclusion. Flake had probably found himself a new, younger, boyfriend, and had been adding to his collection of sex tapes with this virile young man. And when Crier found out, he flew into a rage and killed his lover in a moment of insanity. Classic."

"Right," said Chase. "Sarah and Randal. I want you to talk to the rest of the staff. And ask them about the camera. I'll talk to the head of security." He turned to Odelia. "Are you all right in here, babe?"

Odelia nodded. And when Chase gestured with his head to Gran, she understood his meaning. Not only was she to keep an eye on Leonidas Flake and the crime scene, but also on her grandmother, who was now checking under the bed, as if fully expecting another killer to be holed up there.

Chase and the other police officers walked out and closed the door behind them and then it was just her and Gran and... the dead man.

CHAPTER 7

*I*nstead of joining Odelia and Chase inside the house, as was our habit, we'd instead opted to inspect the outer rim of the Leonidas dwelling. Not that this was part of a new strategy on our part. We were upset with Odelia, and wanted to showcase that annoyance by doing things our way instead of hers. Not that it would do us a lot of good. Humans are notoriously obtuse, and it would take more than the silent treatment for Odelia to become aware of our grievances.

"So what's the plan?" asked Brutus now, and I had to confess that I didn't have any. And since Harriet, usually filled to the brim with plans, was coming up empty in that department, too, and Dooley was, as usual, a spent force when it came to racking the old noggin, we simply wandered around aimlessly, deciding that instead of coming up with a plan to aid and abet our human in solving yet another crime, we were going to go on strike for once.

"On strike?" asked Dooley. "What's a strike, Max?"

"It means we're not going to do what we usually do and instead do nothing at all," I explained.

"Oh, you mean taking a break?"

"No, going on strike," said Harriet. "Like factory workers when negotiations between management and trade unions have broken down and failed to reach the pay raise anticipated."

Dooley stared at me.

"Oh, for crying out loud," Harriet burst out. "We're not going to help Odelia solve her murder for her this time, all right? Instead we do nothing."

Dooley continued mystified, though. "But… why?"

"For one thing, the murder has already been solved," I said. "Clearly the boyfriend did it. And for another, if Odelia doesn't care about us, why should we care about her? Or the murder cases she decides to get involved in?"

This was clearly a tough one, and Dooley stared at me for a moment before responding. "Because that's what we always do?"

"Well, I for one think it's time we switched up our routine," said Harriet. "How long have we been assisting Odelia with this murder business?"

"Um… a long time?" Dooley hazarded a guess.

"Exactly! Too long. We're cats. We're not even supposed to be involved in this crime stuff. What we should do is lie around, have a bit to eat from time to time, or go for a stroll, and generally have a great old time. What we shouldn't be doing, because it is unnatural, and not in our job description, is hunt around for killers. It's dangerous, and it's not a lot of fun."

"Oh, I don't know," said Brutus. "I kinda like hunting around for horrible killers."

"Speak for yourself. I've had enough of this nonsense, and I think going on strike, as Max suggests, is a great idea. In fact I think we should go on an indefinite strike."

"Meaning?" asked Brutus.

"Meaning we hand in our resignation! We tell Odelia that we won't be her flunkeys any longer and that from now on she can find her own killers."

"I don't know if that's such a good idea," said Dooley, always the most conscientious of the lot. "Odelia relies on us to bring her those vital clues she likes so much."

"Well, from now on she'll just have to root around for those vital clues herself, won't she? In fact," she added, getting up from her prostrate position, "I've seen all I need to see of this horrible place. Brutus, let's go home."

And since a suggestion from Harriet always has the ring of finality to it, Brutus had no other choice than to follow her home. Before she turned away, though, she had one last thing to say. "If you two decide to stick around and help Odelia in any way, you're the worst suckers in the history of suckerhood."

"We're not sticking around, are we, Dooley?" I said.

"I don't mind sticking around," said Dooley.

"Of course you don't," said Harriet, a little nastily I thought. "What about you, Max? You're the one who suggested we go on strike."

"I know," I said. "But we just got here, and I don't feel like walking all the way back to the house."

"Well, I do," she said, and beckoned for her mate to follow her.

"Sorry, guys," said Brutus. "Looks like you'll have to go on strike all by yourselves."

I had a feeling Brutus was still a little fuzzy about the whole strike concept, but I didn't feel like explaining it to him, so I merely held up a paw in goodbye, and then Harriet and Brutus were off for a leisurely walk through the outer boroughs of Hampton Cove.

"I'm not sure I want to strike, Max," said Dooley. "Is it difficult?"

"It's very easy," I said. "You simply don't do what you normally do."

He thought hard about this, judging from the thought wrinkles on his brow. "So… we're supposed to be looking around for witnesses of this murder business, right?"

"Right."

"So… going on strike means we don't look for witnesses of the murder?"

"Exactly!"

His face fell. "But then what are we supposed to do? I mean, this striking business seems to be more a lack of activity and not an activity in itself."

"We can simply lounge around out here and wait for Odelia to return and take us back into town. In the meantime we take a nap or something."

"But if she asks what we've discovered, what are we going to tell her?"

"We tell her the truth. That we're on strike and we haven't discovered a single thing."

He gave me a dubious look. "I don't think she'll be happy about that."

"That's the point, Dooley. We show her that we're not happy by not doing what she tells us to do, at which point she'll realize how badly she's been treating us and she'll repent and promise to do better next time."

"And do you think that's going to work?"

"I don't know, Dooley. But we have to try. It's obvious she and Chase are getting ready to leave Hampton Cove and start a new life across the pond, leaving us in the hands of Tex and Marge and Gran. And even though I believe in every individual's right to map their own course in life, I still feel we should express our disappointment and try to persuade her to include us in her plans." Though, truth be told, if Odelia really was planning on leaving us behind, I didn't know if I wanted to be included in her future endeavors. A human capable of betrayal on such a massive scale wasn't the kind of human I wanted to spend the rest of my life with, if you know what I mean.

Dooley seemed to feel the same way, for he now plunked down on the fashion designer's smooth lawn, and heaved a deep sigh as he placed his head on his front paws. "Life is complicated, Max, don't you agree?"

"Yes, I do," I said simply, and lay down on the manicured turf next to Dooley, placing my chin on my paws just like him.

After a moment, he asked, "So are we on strike now?"

"We're on strike," I confirmed.

"Nice," he said. "I kinda like it."

"Me, too, actually. Peaceful."

"Very peaceful."

And in spite of our predicament, we decided to make the best of things by enjoying this rare lull in our busy schedule. And we'd been dozing for the better part of half an hour, the sun warming our weary bones, when a green van came driving up to the house, its tires crunching the gravel. We watched on as it pulled to a full stop and a man came stepping out. He was dressed in a long black overcoat, and had flowing blond hair and a nice blond mustache and beard. On top of his head was a fashionable homburg hat and he was carrying a suitcase. Next, a cat came hopping out of the van. One of those Siamese specimens. Very skinny, but also very loud. So loud we could hear him complaining all the way to where we were lying on Flake's lawn.

"Look at this dump," the cat was saying. "This is beneath us, Chris. Way, way beneath us."

"I know," said the guy. "But a job is a job, buddy, so buck up, will you?"

"How much are they paying us? Cause if it's less than our usual quote I say we get out of here and dump this dump."

"Ten K now, and another ten if we catch her son's killer."

"Twenty K, huh. Not too shabby."

"Yeah, that's what I thought. So are we doing this?"

"Hell, yeah," said the cat.

And cat and man moved towards the front door as one man, then out of sight.

"Weird," said Dooley.

"What's weird?" I asked, closing my eyes again now that the show was over.

"That guy could talk to his cat."

It took me a few moments before realizing the truth in Dooley's worlds. Then my eyes shot open again. "Great Scott, Dooley!" I cried.

"What?"

"That guy can talk to his cat!"

"That's what I said."

"But I always thought Odelia was the only one—and her mom and grandma, of course."

"Well, looks like they're not the only ones," said Dooley sensibly.

I stared at the green van, the engine still ticking as it cooled down. On the side of the car a decal had been stuck. It read 'Christopher Cross—Pet Detective.'

"Competition," I murmured.

"Mh?" asked Dooley, who'd closed his eyes, his favorite strike pose.

"Odelia is getting some serious competition, Dooley."

"So? We're on strike, Max. Officially we've stopped caring about Odelia."

He was right. Officially we didn't care about what happened to Odelia. "Still, I don't think she's going to like it," I said as I rested my head on my paws again.

51

"Maybe it will stop her from taking us for granted," said Dooley.

I smiled. Some people call Dooley dumb. Dooley isn't dumb. A little slow perhaps, but smarter than he often gets credit for. "You're absolutely right, Dooley," I said. "Maybe this is what she needs to stop taking us for granted."

CHAPTER 8

*O*delia was staring out of the window. She felt a little
creeped out by being in the same room as the victim
of a crime. Not that she was particularly squeamish about
being in the presence of a dead person. She'd been involved
in more murder cases than any reporter had a right to be,
especially in a small town like Hampton Cove. But still… It
didn't feel right. Disrespectful, even. Leonidas Flake should
be in the presence of his loved ones. Being laid up in a
funeral home so he could be mourned properly. Not on
display for all the world to see—or at least two amateur
sleuths like herself and Gran.

"Look at this, Odelia," said her grandmother, and she
turned in the direction the old lady was indicating. She was
on hands and knees, poking at something under the bed.

"What is it?" she asked, also getting down on all fours.

"I don't know. Looks like a wrapper."

"A wrapper? Like a candy wrapper?"

"I don't think so. More like the kind of wrapper you use
for a syringe."

"Probably something Flake's nurse dropped."

53

"Yeah, probably. I mean, the guy was old, right? So he probably was prodded and jabbed with a bunch of syringes, like, all the time."

Odelia agreed. Still, just to be on the safe side she took a picture of the item, then shuffled back from under the bed. She was just in time to watch the door swing open and Chase stroll in, followed by the coroner, looking harried.

"Finally," said Gran. "We thought you'd never get here, Abe."

Abe Cornwall was a scruffy-looking man in his mid-fifties with a marked paunch and hair that stuck out in every direction, as if he'd stuck his fingers in a socket. "Another homicide over in Happy Bays," he said as he placed his medical bag on the floor. "Got here as fast as I could. So what have we here?"

"Leonidas Flake," said Gran helpfully. "Designer to the stars. And now up amongst the stars in heaven himself. Unless he's gone straight down to hell, of course. I guess with the kind of life the dude probably led all bets are off."

The coroner stared at Gran for a moment, then proceeded to check the dead man's pulse. "Dead," he said with an air of finality.

"No shit," said Gran. "We didn't need a doctor to tell us that."

Abe gave her a censorious look. "Don't you have someplace to be, Vesta?"

"You ain't getting rid of me that easy, Abe," she said caustically. "Now tell us, did he get whacked, yes or no."

The doctor grumbled something under his breath, then proceeded to pull on a pair of plastic gloves, and give the patient on display his full attention. Moments later, he rose with a serious expression on his face. "Francine will be devastated. She loved his designs."

"Who cares what your wife thinks?" said Gran. "Give us the verdict, medicine man."

"She picked up a nice pair of pants from Costco last month. Two blouses, too. Discounted, of course. Still, she was happy as a clam. Guy knew his stuff."

"Oh, my God! Are you going to keep flapping your gums or are you going to get to the point already?"

"Well, as far as I can tell—and this is very preliminary, mind you—he's been dead for three or four hours. Cause of death is almost certainly a stab wound to the heart. I'll know more once I get him on my slab."

"Thanks, Abe," said Chase, nodding.

"You're welcome. Now if there's nothing else…"

"We found a wrapper for a syringe under the bed," said Gran.

"Probably something his nurse dropped," said the doctor. He moved over to the nightstand and picked through the small collection of medication collected there. "Heart medicine, and diabetes, of course. Hypertension, anxiety… the usual. I'll make you a list if you want."

And as they were about to leave the room, allowing the coroner's people to move the body down to a waiting ambulance and then to the morgue, there was suddenly a commotion at the door and a strange-looking man dressed in a long black overcoat came waltzing in.

"Not so fast," he said, fixing all those present with a steely look.

"And who are you?" asked Chase.

The man drew himself up to his full height. "My name is Christopher Cross. And I was hired by that man's mother," he said, pointing to Leonidas.

All eyes swiveled to the old man on the bed. "Leonidas Flake had a mother?" asked Odelia, voicing the question that had occurred to everyone.

"Yes, he had. She's ninety-eight years old but still in full possession of all her faculties. And upon learning the fate that has befallen her one and only son, she's decided to engage my services."

"And those are…" Gran prompted.

"I'm a private detective, with a long list of accolades and clients, and I'm here to take over this investigation."

"I'm Hampton Cove PD, buddy," said Chase, "so you're not taking over anything."

"Pardon me, sir. Of course I meant taking over from the amateur detectives present." He directed a pointed look to Odelia and Gran. "Odelia Poole, if I'm not mistaken? I thought I'd find you here. And you must be Vesta Muffin. Charmed, I'm sure." And he actually grabbed Gran's hand and tried to press a kiss on it. He would have succeeded if Gran hadn't pulled back her hand and in the process managed to smack the guy across the face with it.

"Ouch," he said, then gave her a nasty look. "If that's the way it's going to be…"

"Look, I don't know what your game is," said Chase, "but this is a police investigation, and this is a crime scene, and you're not invited. So buzz off."

The guy cut a quick glance at the body, then took out his phone and started snapping pictures of the dead body.

"Hey!" said Chase. "What part of buzz off don't you understand?"

"I have an official mandate from the victim's mother," said the detective. "And I will not be bullied!"

Officers Flunk and Skip had returned, and now attached themselves to the man's arms and proceeded to escort him from the room.

"This is an outrage!" the detective was saying. "You'll regret this, Detective Kingsley! Mark my words!"

"Yeah, yeah, yeah," said Chase. "So are we finished here?"

"Yes, we are," said Odelia.

"You can take him away, Doc," Chase told the coroner.

"So what's the verdict?" asked Gran as they left the room. "What did your people find out?"

"Nothing much," said Chase as they descended the stairs. "The maid is the only one who witnessed the aftermath of the crime. We talked to the rest of the staff, and all of them tell the same story: Flake was a very private man, who kept himself to himself. When he was in town he lived here with his boyfriend, and they rarely ventured out. Even though Crier is twenty-five years Flake's junior, the match was a happy one, by all accounts, and they're all shocked Crier could have done what he did. No one expected this."

"Let's hope you find out more when you talk to him," said Gran.

"We will," said Chase. He directed an apologetic look at Odelia. "I'm sorry for dragging you all the way out here."

"That's okay," said Odelia. "I'm glad you won't need my help."

They walked out of the house. "So…" said Chase. "I'm sticking around, to make sure we wrap this up nice and tidy, and to make sure that idiot private detective doesn't give us any more trouble. You two head on back to town."

That idiot detective was at that moment talking to a member of Flake's staff.

"You might tell the guy the case is closed," suggested Gran. "Otherwise he'll only waste Flake's mother a lot of money and his staff a lot of time."

"Oh, he'll drag this out as long as he can," said Chase, giving the man a scornful look. "That's the kind of detective he is."

"You know him?" asked Odelia, surprised.

"I know of him. He's a pet detective. Hired to find missing

pets. Looks like he's stepping up in the world, and tackling the more challenging cases."

They watched the man for a moment, then Odelia decided to look around for her cats. She didn't see any sign of them, though. Odd. And she'd just started calling out their names when a Siamese cat came waddling up to them.

"Look at that furball," said Gran with a grin. "Must be Flake's cat."

"No, it's not," said Chase. "Flake's cat is a Birman and much smaller."

"She's very pretty," said Odelia. "She even has her own Instagram."

The Siamese cat approached them and spoke in a gruff tone. "Hey. You that detective babe?"

Odelia frowned. "Um, I'm a reporter, and sometime detective, yes."

"Tell your cats this case is mine now, you hear?"

"Wait, what?" said Odelia as the cat turned on its paw and snuck into the house.

"You heard," said the cat over his shoulder. "Tell those losers of yours to stay away while I crack this case. And now piss off, will you?"

"Hey, come back here and apologize, you jerk!" Gran shouted, but the cat was gone. "What a shmuck," she said. "Did you hear what he said?"

"Um, no," said Chase. "What?"

Odelia's jaw was still on the floor. No cat had ever spoken to her like that. And when Gran had repeated the cat's words, Chase agreed he was a jerk.

"Let's get out of here," said Gran. "I'm sick to death of this place already."

"Max!" Odelia hollered. "Dooley! We're leaving!"

When no response came, she quickly jogged to the side of the house, but when she saw no sign of her cats, and they didn't respond to more yelling from her part, she finally gave up.

"They're probably halfway home by now," said Gran, who'd joined her.

"Yeah, probably," she agreed.

She got into Gran's car and waved to Chase as they drove off. She couldn't help feeling a slight sensation of unease, though. The same kind of sensation she got when something not-so-good was about to happen.

"I don't like this, Gran," she intimated as her grandmother steered the car along the road back to Hampton Cove.

"Yeah, me neither," said Gran. "No challenge, huh? Way too easy."

"I'm not talking about the case. It's Max and the others. Where are they?"

"Like I said, on their way home. They got a lot less patience than we do, honey. They probably decided half an hour into the thing that it was a big old washout and decided to skedaddle. Cats are a lot smarter than us humans."

Odelia nodded distractedly. In spite of Gran's words she had a very bad feeling. Her stomach was in knots, and not the good kind of knots either.

CHAPTER 9

*C*ats can be difficult. For one thing, we don't like the cold, but neither do we like the heat. Which is why, after having spent an hour soaking up the rays, both Dooley and I felt we needed a change of scenery. So we got up and went in search of a touch of shade, which we found at the back of the house. As is customary in the homes of the rich and famous, we fully expected to find a pool back there, or at the very least a nice jacuzzi. Nothing doing, though. The only thing Mr. Leonidas Flake had indulged in was... a petting zoo.

"Oh, cool!" said Dooley as we found ourselves staring out across a sea of barnyard animals. Even at first glance I could detect a donkey, complete with long ears and a dumb expression on its face, a couple of rabbits, a goat, a flock of sheep, a horse, and even a cow. The whole thing would have excited Noah.

"It sure beats the celebrity penchant for orgies," I said.

"Or drug parties," Dooley added.

As you can well imagine, in the course of our investigations we've seen our fair share of celebrity depravity, and to find a dead celebrity who enjoyed spending time surrounded by barnyard animals was a nice change of pace.

And as we went in search of a place to spend the remainder of our strike, we discovered that one section of the petting zoo was empty. There was the nice little patch of grass, there was the sturdily-built wooden house, and there was the bowl of water, accompanied by a similar bowl filled to the brim with nuggets of food. What there wasn't a trace of was its occupant, whether large or small. So Dooley and I shared a quick glance of understanding, and we moved as one cat into this enclosure, took a sip from the water, took a few bites from the frugal meal, and took a peek inside the little wooden house to see if the owners weren't home by any chance, and when we'd determined to our satisfaction that they weren't, stretched out on the grass and dozed off.

It wasn't until I felt a tickle in my backside that I woke up again. Glancing back, I saw that we'd been joined by... the Siamese cat we'd seen earlier.

"You Max?" the cat asked gruffly.

I answered in the affirmative, happy in the knowledge that my reputation had spread to these faraway parts of Hampton Cove. For a brief moment I experienced what every celebrity must feel like when someone asks for a selfie.

"Just wanted to tell you face to face that your days are numbered, fatso."

I blinked, rudely awakened from my roseate dream of selfie-loving fandom. "Wait, what?" I asked. "What did you just call me?"

"What's going on, Max?" asked Dooley, also waking up from his slumber. I'd never before realized how comforting petting zoos can be. You have your own little space, you have plenty of food and drink, and you get adoring fans who gather round to give you all of their love and affection—

apart from the occasional prod in the ribs with a stick from a wayward child.

"You heard me," growled the Siamese. He directed a nasty look at Dooley. "And you must be Dooley. You look even dumber than I thought you would."

We both stared at him. He wasn't a large specimen, but what he lacked in size he made up for in venom. "Who are you?" I cried, greatly disturbed.

"Name is Tank, and I'm here to tell you that there's a new game in town." He tapped his own chest for some reason. "Move over, bozos. Tank is here."

"Tank?" I asked. "Your name is actually Tank?"

"You don't look like a tank," said Dooley.

"Got a problem with my name?" Tank asked in a challenging, macho way. Like a bully looking for a fight, which I guess he was.

"Oh, no, just an observation," said Dooley.

"Yeah, we never met a cat named Tank before," I said.

"Well, you met him now," Tank growled.

"What do you mean when you say there's a new game in town, though?" asked Dooley. "What game? And which town?"

Tank grinned, displaying some very sharp teeth. "Oh, you are dumb." He tapped my chest, hard. If he'd expected me to roll over, though, he was mistaken. Not because of my extreme courage and superior physical strength, but because of my unique body type. I'm big-boned, you see, and Tank's paw merely disappeared into those big bones of mine, which made a gentle ploinking sound, then wrapped themselves around his paw. Much like Jell-O. Yes, I know most bones aren't made of Jell-O, but mine are, all right?

"My God you are fat!" cried Tank, then tapped my chest again. There was more ploinking and quivering as my body adjusted itself to his touch, and after a while I got quite tired of the whole experience and got up.

He must have been impressed by my sheer size, for he stopped poking me. I may not be strong, or courageous, but what I lack in bravery I make up for in size. Twice the size of Tank, in fact. And even though I'm as docile as a butterfly, size does tend to impress.

He took a step back, and eyed me from beneath glowering brows. "Tell your cronies Harriet and Brutus that from now on I'm the bee's knees, okay? Odelia Poole's reign is over. The name to remember is Christopher Cross."

"I thought it was Tank?" said Dooley, curious.

"Chris Cross and Tank! We're taking over!"

"So who is this Chris Cross?" I asked.

"Don't you play dumb with me, Max," he said, baring his teeth once more. "You know who Chris is—and you know who I am, too."

Dooley and I shared a look, then we both shook our heads. "Never heard of you, I'm afraid," I said.

"Or this Chris Cross person," Dooley added.

"Oh, I see what you're doing. Clever. Very clever. But psyching me out won't work. Chris Cross is the best pet detective in the county—maybe even the country. So it's goodbye to Odelia and Max and hello to Chris and Tank!"

"Hello," said Dooley good-naturedly. "Nice to meet you, Tank." He glanced around. "So where is this Chris?"

"We're taking over the investigation," said Tank, ignoring Dooley. "Just so you know."

"That's all right," said Dooley. "We're on strike anyway."

Tank gave Dooley a strange look, then held up a paw, extended his claws and pretended to slice his own throat for some reason. "Game over," he said, and then he was off, leaving us to stare after him.

"What was that all about?" asked Dooley finally.

"Beats me," I said. "Something about Chris Cross and some game."

"Do you think he understood why we're on strike?" asked Dooley.

"No idea," I said, and I plunked back down again.

"I like this strike thing, Max," said Dooley, closing his eyes.

"I know. You said it before."

"No, but I really like it."

"Me, too, buddy."

"Very relaxing."

"Very."

And then we slept.

CHAPTER 10

*T*he next visitor who swam into our ken wasn't the strangely rude cat who called himself Tank, but a timid white cat who looked as if she'd just seen a ghost. I'd opened one eye at the sound of something or someone slithering through the low grass, and found myself face to face with this new arrival.

"Hey, there," I said good-naturedly, for my mood always improves when I can get some quality shut-eye. Plus, I was happy Tank hadn't returned.

The cat stared at me with fear etched across her furry features. She was a very pretty, smallish cat of the Birman variety if I wasn't mistaken. She also had a little crown on her head and a pendant around her neck that could have been a diamond. My guess was that she lived on the premises. And that her name was Pussy.

"Nice weather we've been having," I said by way of introduction. Always a nice icebreaker. It didn't work on this cat, though, for she continued staring at me as if I were some monster from the deep about to devour her whole.

"Do you live around here?" I asked, going for my second most popular icebreaker.

This time there was a response, as the cat nodded twice.

"Hey, that's great. We're just visiting," I said. "Our human is an amateur sleuth and she's looking into the death of the owner of this place. Did you know him?"

Again a quick nod.

Dooley, who'd woken up from all of my chattering, also opened his eyes.

"Hey there," he said. "Nice weather we've been having."

"Already tried that, Dooley," I said from the corner of my mouth. "No dice."

"Do you live around here?" he asked next.

The cat opened her mouth and said, in a squeaky voice, "I live here. What are you doing in Samson's pen?"

"Samson's pen? Oh, you mean this pen belongs to someone?" I asked.

"Who's Samson?" asked Dooley, deciding to go for the direct approach.

"Samson is Gabe's pet chicken," said the cat, surprising us with her sudden eloquence.

"Pet chicken?" I asked.

She nodded three times. "She ran away last night. I should have known it was a bad sign."

"Chickens do tend to run away," I said, as if I were the world's greatest expert on poultry, which I'm not. I haven't met a lot of chickens in my time, or made friends with our feathered friends. Chickens tend to make themselves scarce when cats are around.

"So where did Samson run off to?" asked Dooley.

The cat shrugged.

"And why is Samson running away a bad sign?" I asked.

"My human died this morning," she said, and looked as if she were on the verge of tears. "And then my other human was arrested for murder, and now it's just me and a dozen staff and who knows what will happen next?"

"I guess the human that's dead will stay dead and the human that was arrested for murder will go to prison," said Dooley. "But that's just a wild guess so don't pin me down on that."

"Dooley!" I hissed. "Can't you see she's distraught."

"Oh, I'm sorry," said Dooley, horrified. "I didn't realize…"

"It's all right," said the cat, her eyes downcast and her lips trembling. "Like I said, I should have seen it coming."

"You mean with Samson running off and all?" I asked.

"Yeah, and with Leo and Gabe fighting all the time."

"Yeah, that's usually a bad sign."

She'd plunked herself down in front of us, and seemed more amenable to chatting now. Always good to get this kind of stuff off your chest. And without boasting I can tell you that both Dooley and I are excellent listeners. That's what you get from living with Harriet and Brutus: they're excellent talkers and we're excellent listeners. And so the world keeps on turning.

"So you're Pussy, right?" I said.

She nodded. "That's me. Lady of the house. Only now I'll probably be foisted off on some relative. I'm not sure I will like that."

"Oh, I'm sure you will," I said, more as a blanket statement of consolation than because I had a clue of the inner workings of the Flake family dynamics.

She gave me a strange look. "I'm worth a great deal of money, you know. So whoever gets me, pretty much wins the lottery."

"Is that right?"

"Well, at least I think I am. Rich, I mean. Leo always said that when he died I would inherit. Not sure if he decided to go through with it in the end."

"From what I heard you inherit the lot," I said. "At least if no will turns up."

"That's... gratifying, I guess," she said. "Though money isn't everything. I'd rather have Leo and Gabe back than to be the richest cat in the world."

"Oh, no, sure," I said, though I had no idea. I've never been the richest cat in the world.

"You also inherit the company," said Dooley.

"Not sure what I'm going to do with it."

"Can cats run a company?"

"I think it might be a little hard. After all, you need to be able to delegate, or get your instructions across, and in this world it's tough to get a human to listen to you, much less do as you say. And then there's the fact that I don't know the first thing about designing, whether for the fall or spring edition."

"Yeah, there's that," I muttered, not a clue what she was talking about.

"Anyway, I'm very glad you decided to listen to me," she said, getting up. "It's nice to have someone to chat with."

"Oh, any time," said Dooley. "We're on strike right now, you see, so we have all the time in the world to listen to all of your gripes and thoughts."

"Thanks," she said softly. "So what are your names?"

"Max," I said.

"Dooley," said Dooley.

"Very nice to meet you, Max and Dooley," she said with a smile.

"Likewise," I said.

"Stick around. I have a feeling Samson isn't coming back, so this pen is yours."

"Thanks for the offer, but we actually have a home."

"Not for long," said Dooley with a sad glance at me.

"Yeah, not for long," I said. "Our human is getting married

soon, and we have reason to believe she's going to chuck us out when she does."

"Oh, that's terrible," said Pussy. "It seems to draw us even closer together, doesn't it? I'm without a human right now, and soon you two will be, too."

We thought about this for a moment, and I had to swallow away a lump. I've never been without a human before, and the prospect didn't appeal to me.

"Maybe we will stay here," said Dooley. "At least for the time being, until Odelia figures out what she wants to do with us."

I nodded my agreement. "We'll hang around," I told Pussy. "We're in the same boat now, and we might as well stick together."

"That's so nice of you," she said, and I could see that the prospect of having a friend in this, her hour of need, greatly bucked her up.

And as she returned to the house, a nice swing in her walk, I thought about the things she'd said.

"Do you really think she'll inherit the Flake fortune?" asked Dooley.

"I doubt it," I said. "Humans may be crazy, but no human is as crazy as that. No, he'll probably have set up some kind of trust fund with Pussy as the beneficiary as long as she lives. She'll be well-provided for."

"Unlike us," said Dooley sadly.

"Unlike us," I agreed.

And as we placed our heads on our paws again, enjoying the hospitality of the absent Samson the chicken, the thought occurred to me that maybe whoever Pussy's new owners were going to be, they might be induced to adopt Dooley and myself and Harriet and Brutus. Unless Marge and Tex and Gran were up to the task, of course. Then again, maybe they weren't. Taking care of one cat is one thing, or even two, but four? Not many humans were prepared to take their love of pets to such an extreme.

And as I drifted off to sleep, the words of Tank came back to me: your reign is over. It very well might be, whatever a reign was.

CHAPTER 11

*L*auren Klepfisch had been watching the house from afar for the better part of the morning, when her trained eye spotted a van arriving and being let through the gate. "Film this," she told her cameraman Zak Kowalski. Zak had been standing slumped against their news van, checking his phone.

He immediately hoisted the camera onto his shoulder and directed it to where Lauren was pointing.

The van carried a decal indicating it belonged to Christopher Cross, Pet Detective, and had a logo of a mean-looking Siamese cat as an added bonus.

Lauren's eyes sparkled as she watched the van drive up to the house, the gate swinging closed behind it. She was a vivacious blonde, and very photogenic, too, which had earned her this job as a correspondent for WLBC-9, Long Island's premier news network—all the news that's fit to broadcast.

Zak put his camera down again. "Pet detective?" he asked. "What the hell is a pet detective?"

"Technically a pet detective is a detective who hunts down missing pets," she said. "But get this. Chris Cross

71

claims he can actually talk to his cat, and has enlisted him in helping find the pets they're looking for. The cat talks to other pets, and relays the information to Cross. They've been at it for years."

"A load of crock, of course."

"I'm not so sure. He does get great results from time to time. He found Lady Delilah's pet canary last month. Silly bird got itself stuck in a chimney."

"Lady Delilah? The pop star?"

"The one and only."

"Lucky for her the cat didn't eat the canary, instead of returning it to its owner."

The gate swung open again and a car came pulling out. Lauren recognized its occupants as Odelia Poole and her grandmother.

"There's a rumor that Odelia Poole can talk to her cat," she said as she watched Odelia drive past without acknowledging her.

"She's the big cheese in town, isn't she? This Odelia Poole?"

"Yeah, she is. Or at least she thinks she is."

"I read her stuff from time to time," said Zak. "Not too shabby."

"Print is a dying medium," said Lauren. "Everybody knows that. And the Gazette's editor is old, so there's no future for an ambitious reporter."

Lauren had built up quite a career as a roving reporter. Burying herself in a town like Hampton Cove the way Odelia Poole had done was not her thing.

"Local news channels are a dying breed too," said Zak. "Online is the future."

"People will always watch local news," she said. "Who else brings the kind of stories that we do? But that doesn't mean I need to stay local, too."

"Ah? Big plans? Do tell."

She smiled. "Not a chance." She liked to play her cards close to her chest. And a notorious blabbermouth like Zak Kowalski was the last person she'd confide in. She had her eye on an anchor position, but as long as no contracts were signed, her lips were sealed. She didn't want to jinx her big break.

"Fine," he said. "So don't tell me." And he went back to playing Tetris on his phone, the only thing he was good at, apart from blabbing.

"Let's get out of here," she said. "The person we need to talk to isn't here anyway."

"So where are they?"

"In jail. And I know just the way we can land ourselves an exclusive."

❧

Odelia and Gran had arrived back in town, and Gran parked the car in front of the doctor's office. "Are you sure you don't need me anymore?" asked Gran as they got out. There was a touch of wistfulness in her voice.

"Yeah, I'm good," said Odelia. "I'll just pop in at the office to write my article and then we can forget all about this nasty murder business."

"Too bad," said Gran with a sigh as she directed a reluctant glance at the door to the doctor's office. "I like a juicy murder mystery from time to time."

"Well, you shouldn't," said Odelia. "Murder mysteries are not meant to be enjoyed, Gran. They're meant to be mourned."

"Oh, but I'm mourning Leonidas Flake," said Gran. "I'm mourning the hell out of that poor man."

After another pregnant pause, in which Odelia kept her

tongue, she finally walked up to the door to the office and disappeared inside. Obviously taking down appointments from people suffering the flu or hemorrhoids was a lot less exciting than hunting down clues and chasing down murderers. Still, Tex needed his receptionist, and Odelia needed her paycheck, so the moment Gran was safely back where she belonged, she walked down the street to the headquarters of the *Hampton Cove Gazette*.

She hadn't lied when she told her grandmother she needed to write her article. What she hadn't mentioned was that she had no intention of dropping the case. Not yet, anyway. Until Leonidas Flake's boyfriend had confessed to the crime of murdering his partner, there was still a chance that new developments might swing the case in a different direction altogether. Chances of that happening were very slim, of course, but she'd investigated enough crimes by now to know that things are not always what they seem.

Though in this case it looked very bad for Gabriel Crier. Very bad indeed.

She walked into the office and greeted Dan, who was ensconced in his office, furiously typing away on his computer. He looked up when Odelia strode in.

"Oh, hey there," he greeted her cheerfully. "So how were things at *Le Chateau Flake*?"

"Pretty straightforward," she said as she took a seat on the leather couch that Dan kept in his office for visitors. "Flake was killed with a single stab to the heart, and his boyfriend was seen with the knife in his hand, standing over the body of his dead lover."

"Too bad," said Dan, shaking his head. "I liked this Flake fellow. Contrary to some of the other celebrities that consider Hampton Cove their second home, he actually had a gift, and made this world a more beautiful place."

"I've never heard you get lyrical over a celebrity before, Dan," said Odelia, surprised. "Did you know the guy well?"

Dan, a weathered-looking man in his late sixties with a long white beard, nodded. "He used to come into the office from time to time and we'd share a glass. Did you know he loved animals? Always told me that if he hadn't become a designer he would have been a vet. He sometimes thought he might become one yet, if and when he decided to retire from creating the most gorgeous garments imaginable. Of course he was never going to retire."

"And now he'll never be a vet," said Odelia.

Dan, who loved animals himself, perked up at the chance to hold forth on one of his favorite topics. "He once invited me to check out his petting zoo. He had all sorts of pets, and not the exotic ones either. He would never imprison an animal if he could help it. Only kept the barnyard variety. Eccentric fellow. Very eccentric, with very strong ideas on all sorts of topics. He'll be missed."

"He'll also be missed by all the people who watched his shows, or bought his designs." She herself had never been into couture, haute or low. Too expensive and too impractical. She was more a jeans-and-T-shirt sort of girl, though she did love a nice pair of exclusive Converse and had a modest collection at the house. And if she were as rich as Leonidas Flake, she might take an interest in fashion, and start spending serious money on her outfit. On a reporter's salary that simply wasn't possible, but she was okay with that.

Dan had taken a whiskey bottle from his desk drawer and now poured a finger into a glass, then offered her one.

"No, thanks," she said, holding up her hand. "I need to finish the Flake piece."

"Have you talked to Crier?"

"Chase and Uncle Alec will interview him."

"Good luck with that."

"You know something I don't?"

"Only that Gabe Crier is a cryer. The man cries for the least little thing. When he sees a newborn baby—waterworks. When he watches *Will & Grace*—same thing. Leo used to complain that living with Gabe was like living life on an emotional roller coaster. Every high was followed by an even deeper low."

"So why did he stay with him?"

Dan raised his glass. "He said Gabe had... other qualities." He quirked a meaningful eyebrow, and Odelia got the message.

Retreating to her office, she wondered briefly where Max and the others could be. By now they should have had the chance to talk to Pussy, Flake's famous cat. If only to add another angle to her story. But then she relaxed. Gran was right. They'd probably returned home by now. Or maybe, just maybe, they were still scouting the Flake place. Max liked to be thorough when he was investigating a crime. He was probably still hard at work, extracting information from Pussy. And if Flake really had a petting zoo, they would have found plenty of witnesses to talk to. Good thing she had until tonight to finish her story. She'd find Max when she got home, get a few juicy quotes, sprinkle them into her story, then send it to Dan for his final edit.

She took out her phone and brought up Pussy's Instagram. She was an exceedingly pretty cat, and her feed showcased her expensive habits: gorgeous haircuts, fancy outfits, exclusive parties, funky playpen, gourmet pâté...

She smiled. No wonder Max and the others had vanished from the face of the earth. They were probably having the time of their life with Princess Pussy.

CHAPTER 12

hen I say that cats, as a rule, don't like it when things get too hot or too cold, I like to include myself in that description. The sun had gradually risen, and had kept on rising, and had now reached the point where it had hoisted itself over the roof of the monstrosity that Leonidas Flake had built. And showcasing its customary playfulness, it now tickled my nose, and soon I was hotting up to such an extent that, even though the grass was still cool, I was getting increasingly uncomfortable. Dooley must have reached the same conclusion, for he opened his eyes at the same time I did, and said plaintively, "This darned sun keeps following us wherever we go, Max. It's persecution."

I could have told him that the sun in actual fact did no such thing. That the earth revolves around the sun and not the other way around, but I was too lazy from my nice nap to bother. So all I said was, "Let's find another spot."

But as soon as we got up we both experienced a little hunger, so instead of relocating we decided instead to follow in our ancestors' paw steps and go in search of a bite to eat instead. Even though Samson the chicken might have enjoyed the food he'd been given, I have to admit it left much to be desired.

So we set paw for the house, the only place we hadn't examined, since we were still on strike.

"We can sneak into the house and not break our strike, can't we, Max?" asked Dooley as we approached that ominous block of black concrete.

"Of course," I said. "The only thing we can't do is perform acts of detection. So no talking to any suspects or witnesses or whatever."

"I can do that," said Dooley cheerfully.

As we moved away from the petting zoo, a deep voice rang out behind us. "Hey, cats!" the voice spoke.

We both turned, and discovered the voice belonged to the donkey.

"Yes, donkey?" I said politely, for Odelia has always taught us to be polite.

"Is it true that you're some kind of detectives?"

"No, we're not," I said. "Well, technically we are," I admitted when Dooley gave me a curious look, "but right now we're on strike so we're not allowed by our union to perform any detective-related activities."

The donkey was silent while he absorbed this important information, then said, "Is it true that the boss is dead?"

"Yes," I said, not seeing how confirming the man's death broke the union decree. "Yes, he is. At least that's what a usually reliable source told us."

"How did he die?"

"Stabbed in the chest. By his live-in lover, a man called…"

"Gabriel Crier," said the donkey somberly. "I know Gabe. We all do."

More animals had gathered around. I saw a horse, a cow, a goat, two rabbits, two sheep… Quite the collection.

"I liked Leonidas," said one of the rabbits. "He always gave me fresh grass and hay. Who's going to give me fresh grass and hay now?"

"I'm sure someone else will come along to take care of you all," I said. "By all accounts Mr. Flake was a very wealthy man and I'm sure he'll have made provisions for you in his last will and testament."

"I'll bet he didn't," bleated the goat, who seemed like a somber sort of fellow. "I'll bet he forgot all about us."

"I'm sure he didn't," countered the donkey. "I actually asked Gabe about it last week."

"And what did he say?"

"Well, always considering the fact that Gabe doesn't actually speak donkey, the impression I got was that he cares for us a great deal and would never leave us to fend for ourselves."

"What does that even mean?!" cried the cow.

"It means that he will have made sure we'd be taken care of."

"But he's in jail, isn't he? For murder!" said the sheep. "So if he's gone, and the old man's gone, who's going to need me? Who's going to feed me?"

Somehow this reminded me of a song, though I couldn't quite place my finger on it.

All the animals now started talking across one another, and things were getting a little heated. So Dooley and I decided to withdraw. We were still on strike, so there was very little we could do for these poor creatures. And as we walked in the direction of the house, Dooley said, "So sad, right, Max?"

"Yes, very sad," I said.

"Poor animals. They'll probably end up being sold to the highest bidder."

"Or end up like Bubbles."

"Bubbles?" he asked.

"Michael Jackson's chimpanzee. He was a global celebrity back in the eighties and nineties, until he got too big and unruly, and he was transferred to a sanctuary for chimps and orangutans."

"Is that's what's going to happen to us, Max?"

"I'm sure provisions will have been made…" I began, then realized what I was saying. We shared a glance. "Whatever happens," I said, "we can always turn to the streets, and go and live with Clarice."

"Clarice scares me, Max."

"I know. She scares me, too. But she won't let us die of hunger or thirst. She'll take care of us if need be."

"By feeding us rats! Like she did with Brutus, remember?"

"She meant well," I said.

Once when Brutus was in the dumps, he'd adopted the street life, and Clarice had come through for him, by leaving him the best and juiciest rat she could find behind the dumpsters she considered her personal feeding bowl.

I shivered, and thought of the delicious kibble Odelia always provided us with, and the wet food from those aluminum pouches she liked to buy.

"Too bad humans are so untrustworthy," said Dooley.

"I hear you, buddy."

We'd arrived at the deck that had been constructed at the back of the house, and looked for a way in. We finally found one when we discovered someone had left a window open. A burly guard stood sentry—probably part of a collective of burly guards protecting the place against burglars or sensation seekers. He didn't take any notice of us so we entered the house.

The place was huge, albeit a little sparsely furnished. The floors were all concrete, as were the walls and the ceilings.

"Very modern," said Dooley appreciatively.

"I guess," I said as I studied a very large portrait of

Leonidas Flake that adorned one wall. It was a black-and-white painting of the famous designer only dressed in a leopard-print G-string and his trademark large sunglasses.

"Huh," was Dooley's only comment as he took in the arresting image.

Like the painting, the rest of what I assumed to be the living room was also dominated by the same color scheme: black and white. Very... soothing.

"We need to find the kitchen," I said. "Or Pussy."

So we both stuck our noses in the air and sniffed for a hint of either food or Pussy or both. Soon I'd picked up the scent of the Instafamous cat, and we trotted in the direction my powerful sense of smell told me to go. We passed through another sparsely furnished room, this one looking like a study or a library, with plenty of books (all black and white spines) and another room that only held two pianos: one black and one white. Frankly my eyes were starting to hurt.

We finally entered a room at the end of a long corridor that was filled with the kind of paraphernalia only cats would enjoy: plush animals, scratching posts, climbing trees, balls and tunnels... An overpowering smell of catnip filled the air but, like the other rooms, everything was in black and white.

"Where's the color, Max?!" asked Dooley, on whom the lack of hue was starting to weigh, too. "Is it my eyes? Is everything black and white, or is it just me?"

"It's not just you. I don't see any color, either."

"We're color-blind!"

I held up my paw in front of his face. "What color is this?"

"Um... orange?"

"Blorange," I corrected him, and was gratified to see a smile light up his face.

"I can still see color! I'm not color-blind."

"No, you're not. It's this house. Someone has removed all the colors."

Just then, Pussy came shuffling into the room, looking distinctly depressed. She halted in her tracks when she saw us. "Hey, you guys," she said, perking up. "What are you doing here?"

"Oh, we just thought you'd appreciate some company," I said.

"Food," said Dooley, who's not the diplomat I am. "We're hungry."

Pussy nodded mournfully, as if the topic of food disgusted her, but she could still understand where we were coming from. "Follow me," she said.

"Has this house always been like this?" I asked, gesturing to the endless piles of black-and-white plush animals.

"Like what?" she asked.

"Devoid of color?"

She nodded sadly. "Leo only liked black and white and shades of gray. He hated color."

"Must be a terrible way to live."

"It is—or was. Once Gabe gave me an orange Garfield and Leo bust a nut when he saw it. He made Gabe send it back to the store and have it replaced with a gray Garfield. It's not the same thing."

"No, it's not," I agreed.

"I can't imagine a gray Garfield," said Dooley. "Garfield should be orange."

"Yeah, he should," said Pussy. She was dragging her heels as if the weight of the world rested on her slender shoulders. Finally we passed the stairwell: concrete stairs set in a concrete wall, and then finally into the kitchen—all concrete floors and walls and plenty of gleaming steel. "In here," she said.

We now found ourselves in a side kitchen, completely

devoted to Pussy and her needs. There were large plastic bins hooked to the far wall, with some kind of receptacles below.

"Just follow my lead," she said, and pushed her snout against what looked like a lever. A few pieces of kibble came dropping down into the receptacle and she gave us a sad look as if saying: Well, there you go. "All the different types of kibble are here," she said with as much zip and zest as a funeral home director. "You've got your chicken, your turkey, your rabbit... And if you want brands, you'll find them all there—every label under the sun."

What fascinated me, though, was that all the kibble consisted of different shades of gray.

"Don't tell me Leo got the kibble painted gray," I said, amazed.

"Yeah, he got the stuff specially made by the manufacturers. They cooked up batches of the stuff just for him—or me, I guess."

"Jeez," I said, but still eagerly thumped my snout against one of the levers of what looked like prime gourmet kibble, and out tumbled several nuggets. I eagerly gobbled them up, then spewed them out again. "Yuck!" I said. "What is this flavor?"

"Ash, I guess," said Pussy. "Leo didn't believe in flavor. Or smell. He said we needed to get rid of our unnatural attachment to taste. He liked a clean palate, so his imagination could run rampant. He didn't like color, or taste, or beautiful music or anything that could interfere with his ability to create."

"Oh, my Lord," I said, eyeing the poor cat with unadulterated pity. "What a sad, sad life you must have lived."

"Hey, at least I'm one of the richest cats in the world," she said without enthusiasm.

"Well, your days of living life without taste or color or sound or smell will be over now, right?" I said.

"Wanna bet?" she said. "With my luck I'll probably end up living with someone even worse than Leo."

We ate in silence, and even though the stuff was utterly tasteless and odorless, I still ate my fill. The stomach wants what it wants, right?

And here I thought I knew how the other half lived, I thought as I watched Pussy drink from what looked like a silver salver filled to the brim with crystal-clear water— probably sterilized, if the rest was any indication.

"You should stick around," said Pussy finally. "There's going to be a big meeting tonight. All the important people are going to be there."

"What important people?" I asked.

"Oh, I don't know. Lawyers and board members and shareholders and executives and such. I'll bet they'll decide my fate at the meeting, so I probably shouldn't miss it for the world, but…" She hesitated and gave me a forlorn look. "Could you do me a great, big, gigantic favor?"

"Anything," I said.

"Could you attend the meeting for me? And then tell me what they decided?"

"I don't understand."

"It's too much for me," she said. "I'm sure these are pretty horrible people. As lifeless and colorless and soulless as the rest of this place. And I simply can't bear to listen to them while they discuss my future. I need you to tell me about the parts that are important for me to know. Only the facts."

"Sure, no problem," I said. "But aren't they going to notice us and kick us out?"

"No, they won't," she said with a wan smile. "You'll see."

And with these mysterious words she left us.

"How very sad," said Dooley.

"Yeah," I said. "And to think that I actually used to envy

her. When we watched her Instagram pictures I always thought she had it made."

"Me too," said Dooley. "The richest, most spoiled cat in the world. Poor, poor Pussy."

"Poor Pussy," I agreed, and then gobbled up some more kibble. It was utterly tasteless and odorless, but it still hit the spot, especially since I hadn't eaten anything since that morning.

"So we'll stick around and listen in on this meeting?" Dooley asked.

"I think we owe it to Pussy, don't you?"

"Isn't this against union rules?"

"I don't think so. It's got nothing to do with the case, right? We're only doing this as a personal favor to Pussy."

So we ambled out of the kitchen, and then went for a ramble around the house. Pussy, who'd returned from a short interlude in the bathroom to act as our tour guide, showed us all the best spots where she liked to lay her weary head, and invited us to enjoy them. It was the nicest thing any cat had ever done for us. Usually cats hate it when other cats invade their space, or even dare to come near their favorite spots, but Pussy had no qualms. What struck me, after we passed through several of the bedrooms and a couple of the bathrooms, was that life at Chateau Leonidas must have been pretty lonely for her, and quite dull. Maybe Leo and Gabe had loved her, and spoiled her rotten, but she still seemed unhappy. And suddenly I felt a little homesick, and started to long to be home again, snuggling up to Odelia on the couch while watching some silly show. Dooley must have felt the same way, for he gave me a sad glance that offered a glimpse into his soul. That glimpse was like a mirror: once Odelia was married, our lives would never be the same again.

But then I steeled myself. I was not going to allow myself

to become prey to my emotions. It was the house, I suddenly realized, and Pussy's mood, infecting me with their sadness and melancholy.

So I decided to perk up, and enjoy these rare Instagramable moments.

CHAPTER 13

Uncle Alec and Chase watched the man sitting across from them at the table and Alec wondered when he'd last seen a more miserable piece of human than this guy. Gabriel Crier was a well-preserved quinquagenarian with gentle features and close-cropped hair of a light blond hue. Right now, though, he had dark circles under his eyes, and his tan skin was blotched.

"But I'm telling you, I didn't do it," he repeated not for the first time.

"There's a witness, Gabriel," said Alec. "One of the maids saw you, with the knife in your hand, and blood all over your shirt."

"I know," he said, shaking his head. "I was there, remember? But I'm still telling you I couldn't have done it. I loved Leo. I would never…"

"So what do you think happened?" asked Chase, who had more patience than Alec.

"I don't know, but I can't have killed him. I would never… would I?"

"Is it true you and Leonidas had a big fight last night?"

Gabriel placed his hands on his head and nodded. "We did."

"Can I ask what the fight was about?"

"The same as usual. I wanted Leo to take a step back—to relinquish the reins—basically to retire, and he flat-out refused. I told him he was seventy-eight and had earned the right to rest on his laurels. I wanted us to spend more time together. Travel the world. He was in excellent health and we'd been talking about spending a couple of months in Asia. Leo loved Malaysia, and always wanted to visit but his work prevented him. So I told him to leave the heavy lifting to his staff and take a step back but he insisted he couldn't stop now."

"Why not?" asked Alec. "I mean, like you said, he was seventy-eight. If he didn't retire now when was he going to?"

"I don't know. He claimed that things at the company were such that he simply couldn't afford to assume a more hands-off role."

"Things at the company were bad, you mean?" asked Chase.

"No idea. I'm not a business person myself. I used to be Leo's hairstylist. That's how we met, and then soon after I became his personal stylist and things progressed from there. I also used to do massages on the side. But that didn't exactly make me qualified to determine what was going on at Leonidas Flake. All I know is that poor Leo was under a lot of pressure, which is why I told him to consider retirement or at least to take a break. But he refused, and said that if he stepped down as president and CEO now the whole house of cards could very well collapse and then everything he'd worked for would be reduced to nothing. I didn't understand. How can an empire like Leonidas Flake collapse simply because the founder decides to retire? There must be plenty of people who can run that business, right?"

"I don't know, buddy," said Alec, who felt sorry for the guy, in spite of the fact that he was obviously a killer. "I'm not really into fashion myself."

"Leo had trained a lieutenant. A second-in-command and potential successor. Xavier Yesmanicki. He'd been running the day-to-day side of the business for years, and was ready to take over. Or at least that's what Leo told me. He was so proud of Xavier. Said that if only he'd found him sooner he'd have been able to make Leonidas Flake twice as big as it was now. Anyway, our arguments always revolved around the same topic: I saw that he was suffering and so I urged him to slow down, and that made him upset, and so he threw in my face that all I wanted was to destroy his life's work and yadda yadda yadda." He threw his hands in the air. "It was horrible. Horrible!"

"And so one thing led to another and in a fit of rage you killed him."

"No! When I get upset I don't lash out. That's not in my nature. I simply… crawl into my shell and completely… shut down, I guess." His lip trembled as he nervously touched it. "I guess it's the way I'm built—I don't know."

"So you gave him the silent treatment."

"Yes, I did! Because it's what I always do. We don't speak for a day, maybe two days, and then we get up in the morning and we both act as if nothing happened, and then finally we hug it out and there will be tears and apologies and remorse and…" He blushed. "Well, make-up sex is popular for a reason."

"Only this time there was no make-up sex," said Chase.

He groaned and buried his face in his hands. "This is a nightmare! This is a horror show! My life is ruined! And who's going to take care of Pussy now?"

Alec shuffled uneasily in his chair. This interview wasn't going well.

"So where is Pussy now?" he asked.

"Back at the house. Oh, she'll get all the food and water she needs, but it's the *affection* she'll miss. The *love* she gets from her papas." He was rocking back and forth, hugging himself. "Poor Pussy. She *needs* her papas."

"I'm sure Pussy will be fine," said Chase. "Now let's go back to last night. So you and Leo had a fight."

"A very big fight."

"So you…"

"So I walked out and went into my room, slamming the door. Then I put my music on as loud as possible. Rihanna, of course. Or it could have been Beyoncé. I don't remember. Leo hated music. He said it messed up his frequency."

"His frequency?"

"His body's vibrational frequency. He had this theory that all creation comes out of the void—out of nothingness. So he needed to create a void in himself. Nothingness. No smell, no color, no taste, no sound… He would even put on gloves to cut out his sense of touch. Turn off the light. Meditate for hours and hours. And out of this nothingness, pure creation would ensue."

"Well, he did create a pretty big business empire," said Chase, "so maybe he was onto something."

"I don't think so. I think Leo was damaged. He had a horrible childhood, with parents who never showed him an ounce of affection. It made him bitter and withdrawn. He lived like the proverbial boy in the bubble, only his bubble was self-created."

"And then you entered that bubble," said Alec.

"Yes, I entered the bubble. Oh, don't get me wrong, Leo wasn't antisocial. He had lots of friends, and he liked to have fun. Just not when he was working."

"I see. So back to last night. You were in your room, listening to Rihanna."

"Or Beyoncé," Chase added helpfully.

"I blasted my music all through the house at full volume. Five minutes later he came stomping into my room and yanked the speaker from the wall, then threw it out the window!" He laughed, then cried. "It was the last time I saw him! My beautiful, darling boy!"

"So how do you explain you standing at the side of the bed with a knife in your hand?"

"That's just it! I can't! I was asleep in my bed. Took me hours to fall asleep, worried as I was about Leo, and the fight we had. When we fight I always sleep badly. And then suddenly I'm wide awake, and I'm standing over him, and there's blood everywhere, and there's something cold and metallic in my hand and-and-and... Leo is dead, staring up at me with those lifeless, accusing eyes! As if he knew what I did and he wanted me to know that he knew!" He broke down, and Alec shook his head. They weren't getting anywhere with this guy. So he and Chase got up and walked out to confer.

"Either he doesn't remember or he's a great actor," said Chase.

"He seems sincere," said Alec. "But it doesn't matter. He was there—he did it. No jury will think otherwise, and no judge will decide not to convict him."

Chase stared through the one-way mirror into the room where their suspect still sat, rocking back and forth again, his arms wrapped around himself and his face turned up to the ceiling, crying bitter tears.

"I feel sorry for the guy, though," he said.

"He probably just lost it. Felt abandoned, or angry, flew into a rage. It happens, especially with emotional types like him. They bottle up their emotions for a while, then erupt like a geyser." When Chase gave him a look of amusement, he said, "What?!"

"Is that your professional opinion, Mr. Freud?"

"The hell should I know! But it stands to reason he must have been out of it, made a grab for the knife, and stabbed. And that's all it took, unfortunately. And when he finally came to, it was too late. The boyfriend was dead."

"Diminished responsibility?"

"That's for the judge to decide. I'm just telling it like I see it."

There was a commotion behind them, and suddenly a blond-haired woman came bursting into the room, accompanied by a man with a camera, and before they could stop them they were aiming the camera at their suspect and the woman was firing off a barrage of questions at the Chief.

"Hey! Get the hell out of here!" he yelled.

Dolores, the police station receptionist, came huffing in. "I tried to stop them, Chief!" she cried. "They pushed right past me!"

"Is Gabriel Crier the killer, Chief? Why did he do it?" asked the woman. "And is it true that Leo Flake left his entire fortune to his cat? Any comment?"

"Get out!" thundered the Chief. "Out! Out! Out!"

More officers had arrived on the scene, and managed to muscle the twosome out of the room before their chief had a conniption fit.

"Can you believe that?" he demanded hotly.

"Actually, I can," said Chase, who seemed amused at the interlude.

And as Alec stood reeling, he remembered the woman reporter's last question: Is it true that Flake is leaving his entire fortune to his cat?

"Well, I'll be damned," he said. "Maybe that's our motive, buddy. If Flake had decided to leave everything to his cat, then maybe this made Crier so angry he decided to kill him."

"Which means he'll get nothing," said Chase. "Not much of a motive, Chief."

"Yeah, I guess you're right," he said, frowning as he tapped his lip with his index finger. "We're not talking about a rational person, here, though, Chase. And he might be lying about the fight. They could have been fighting over the inheritance, not about Leo Flake being a workaholic."

"Let's get back in there and have another crack at the guy," Chase suggested.

They both joined Gabriel Crier in the interrogation room once more, and this time Alec decided to change tack. Instead of being the nice cop, he decided to play the bad cop and go for broke.

So he pounded the table with his fist—hard. "Isn't it true that you and Leo fought about his intention to leave his fortune to his cat?" he demanded.

Gabriel stared at him, the sudden change in the chief's demeanor shocking.

"N-n-no," he said feebly. "No, like I said, we—"

"You couldn't stand that he would leave everything to his cat and nothing to you, could you!" the Chief roared, pounding the table three times in quick succession and causing Gabriel to flinch. "And *that's* why you fought! And *that's* why you killed him, because you were so angry you felt you had nothing to lose!"

"N-n-no! I l-l-loved him. He l-l-loved me. The Pussy thing was simply a way for him to... Oh, Christ. Look, he left everything to Pussy, but he also left Pussy to me, so in a roundabout way he left everything to me, you see."

"Bullshit!" cried Alec, then wondered why he'd said that.

Chase, deciding to take over, said, "'So is that why you killed him, Gabriel? Because you wanted to lay your hands on all of that money?"

"No! I wasn't with him for the money. I was with him for

93

love. And I wanted him to live forever, and he could have, for he was in great shape. He was probably in better shape than me, in spite of his age. Look, you have to look into this," he said, nervously searching Chase's face. "You really have to. The more I think about it, the more convinced I am that I didn't do this. I know myself. I'm not a killer. Whenever we had a spider in the bathroom I'd yell for Leo. I can't even swat a fly, or a wasp—or a mosquito! And I definitely can't kill a human being—or my beloved, lovely Leo!"

"But you did," Alec pointed out. "And all we need to know is why. But even so, you're still going to be convicted of this crime, Gabriel, so you might as well talk."

"Oh, God," said Gabriel, and thumped his head on the table.

"Hey, Gabriel, hey, hey, hey," said Alec, realizing he might have taken this bad cop routine too far. "It's fine. I'm sorry I yelled at you, okay? I'm sorry."

Chase arched his eyebrows. 'You're the worst bad cop in the history of bad cops,' his expression seemed to say.

"Listen, buddy," said Alec, placing his hand on the man's shoulder. "We'll investigate further, all right? But it's not looking too good for you, you do see that, right?"

Gabriel lifted his head from the table, a big red welt on his forehead. It contrasted nicely with the pallor of the rest of his face. "It doesn't look too good for me," he repeated automatically, then added, "Someone is trying to frame me, Chief. There's no other possibility."

"Or you killed him and blocked it out," said the Chief gently.

Gabriel blinked. "Yeah," he said finally. "I guess that's also possible."

CHAPTER 14

*O*delia arrived home a little after six. She'd written the biggest chunk of her article for the paper but there were still a few gaps in the story she needed to patch up. She hoped Max and the others would have sniffed out a few choice tidbits of intel, straight from the horse's mouth, or, if a horse hadn't been available, some other animal. The petting zoo should have supplied plenty of material to work with. Those little details that give a story oomph and that *je-ne-sais-quoi* your average reader is looking for when picking up his morning paper or checking his morning website, as nowadays was more the habit.

The *Hampton Cove Gazette* had been around for such a long time it had become an institution in the home of Hampton Covians, and with a little help from the newspaper gods it would remain that way for a good long time to come. Even though Dan was getting on in years, he wasn't about to retire any time soon, and even if he was, his succession was assured in the form of Odelia, his number-one lieutenant.

Thinking about succession, Odelia suddenly wondered

what the deal with Pussy would be now that she was officially the head of the company. And with Gabe in jail, who the person in charge of her care would be. She'd been searching online but had found precious little information in that regard. Vowing to talk to her future hubby, who had, no doubt, in the course of his fireside chats with Flake's killer, gleaned that morsel of info and then some, she hurried into the house, eager to interview man and beast in the service of her article.

The first living form she met was Chase, draped across the sofa and reading on his phone.

"Hey, babe," he said as she came hurrying in. "Did you finish your article?"

"Not yet," she said as she took a seat across from him. "Now tell me all about what happened with Gabriel. Did he do it, and if he did, why did he do it, and if he didn't, why was he standing over his lover's dead body with a bloodied knife in his hand and a murderer's dazed look in his eyes?"

"Well, he claims he didn't do it, though he's not entirely sure, and he concedes that it's not looking too good for him," Chase revealed, with the easygoing manner of the first party who knows all and is about to impart some of his secrets to a deserving second party.

"So he thinks he didn't do it but he admits he might have done it?"

"Something like that. Your uncle went full bad cop on him but instead of folding the man simply burst into tears and stuck to his guns. He has no recollection of what happened. One minute he was sound asleep in his bed, and the next he was standing there, the image of the crazed killer."

"Huh."

"It's possible he's lying, of course, though he didn't give me that impression. "

"He could have done it and then blocked out the memory."

"Possible, though it will probably take a psychologist to dig that out of his subconscious."

"Is it possible he didn't do it? That someone else planted that knife in his hand?"

"How? The man was there. He wasn't sleepwalking."

Odelia thought about this. "He could have been. Or someone could have put something in his drink that made him lose consciousness."

Chase shook his head. "In my experience the most plausible explanation is usually the right one, babe. The man was there, and he more or less confessed, and even if he doesn't remember we have enough evidence to get a conviction."

"So case closed?"

"As far as your uncle is concerned, case closed, and I doubt whether a judge will think otherwise."

She glanced around. "Where are my cats?"

He picked up his phone again. "Haven't seen them, actually."

She got up and went in search of her feline brood. "Maxie," she said, checking the kitchen, then shouting up at the bottom of the stairs, "Max? Dooley? Are you guys up there?"

When no response came, Chase shouted from the living room, "Maybe they're outside. I think I saw Harriet in the backyard when I got home—or at least a flash of something white and fluffy."

She walked to the sliding glass door and stepped out onto the deck. "Max? Dooley? Harriet? Brutus? Anyone?"

Suddenly a white head came peeking from beyond the tulip tree at the back of the garden. It was a favored spot for her cats, especially Harriet and Brutus, who'd turned it into some sort of lovers' lane—minus the lane.

The white head immediately retracted but Odelia headed

over there, wondering about the sudden coyness of her cats. Usually when she arrived home they were at the door, welcoming her, or complaining loudly that she'd arrived so late and had left them to their own devices.

"Harriet?" she said. "Is that you?" When no response came she went down on hands and knees and checked underneath the foliage. "I know you're in there, honey. Is Max with you?"

Finally, realizing the gig was up, and playing hide and seek would no longer serve her purpose, whatever it was, Harriet emerged, followed by Brutus. "No, Max isn't here," she said, a little coldly. "Nor will you find him on the premises. At least not as long as he doesn't want to be found."

This was getting curiouser and curiouser. "What do you mean? Why would Max not want to be found?"

"We're on strike," said Brutus.

"Shush, Brutus, "said Harriet.

"Oh, I didn't know it was a secret," said Brutus.

"It's not a secret, per se," Harriet admitted, "but it's better Odelia finds out for herself."

"You're on strike?" said Odelia, wondering what her cats were up to this time. "Why?"

"That's for us to know and for you to find out," said Harriet, acting her usual prissy self.

"Not enough attention," said Brutus, who seemed more forthcoming with information than his mate.

"Brutus!"

"What? She's going to find out soon enough anyway, so why not tell her what's going on?"

"She knows perfectly well what's going on. She simply prefers to play dumb," said Harriet, giving Odelia a nasty look.

"Well, I don't get it," said Odelia, taking a seat on the lawn. She moved aside a rubber ball and a garden gnome Gran had put there for the cats' entertainment. "Now tell me all, please, because I'm not getting it."

"If you don't get it, maybe you should think about it a little more," said Harriet.

"Oh, for crying out loud," said Odelia, throwing up her hands. "Tell me what's going on already, will you?"

"Fine," said Harriet, then pressed her lips together and gave her partner in crime a look that said, 'You tell her.'

"We feel that you've been ignoring us lately," said Brutus, taking the plunge.

"You told me about that in the car, remember? And I apologized and said I was sorry and you said you each needed twelve percent of my time and I was ready to agree to that in writing when we got interrupted."

"Well, we feel you're not taking our negotiations seriously so we decided to go on strike," said Harriet. "So there will be no more sleuthing on your behalf until you tell us what you're up to."

"Up to?"

"Oh, don't play dumb, Odelia!" said Harriet. "We know very well that you're about to get married and as soon as you do you and Chase will move away—possibly to England, possibly to New York—and you'll dump us!"

"Oh, honey, no!" said Odelia, part horrified, part amused.

"Max seems to think you'll move to England," said Brutus, "but for my money it's more likely you'll move to New York. Chase has family there, after all, so that would be the logical thing to do."

"And it would suit your ambitions to become an ace reporter for an ace newspaper, and not the local rag you bust your gut at now," Harriet added.

"And Chase could join the NYPD again," said Brutus.

"Oh, my sweet, sweet babies," said Odelia, genuinely

touched by this outpouring of concern. "No! Of course I'm not moving away."

"You're not?" asked Brutus, suspicious.

"No! We're staying put, wedding or no wedding. Besides, it's not that we're anxious to tie the knot any time soon. It could be months or years before we finally get hitched."

"But Chase proposed. In London," Harriet pointed out." So that has to mean something. Humans don't just propose and then break it off again."

"He proposed while under attack. I guess you could say it was one of those moments where you see your life flashing by, and you realize there are so many things you haven't done yet."

"Like getting married?"

"Like getting married," she said with a smile.

"So Chase proposing was just a joke?" asked Brutus hopefully. "A fun little joke?"

"It wasn't a joke. He meant it at the time, and I meant it when I said yes, but that doesn't mean we have to rush into things. I'm sure that eventually we will get married, but we're not in any hurry here. And we're not planning to move away from Hampton Cove, or this house. I love it here, and I love living next door to my mom and dad."

"And Gran," Brutus supplied.

"And Gran," she said after a pause. "So even after we're married we'll stay right here. This is your home, you guys, and we're not about to take that away from you. And if I paid less attention to you than usual, I'm sorry. It's just that, when you've gone through a terrible experience like the one we had in England, you realize how precious life is, so we decided to go on all the dates we always wanted to go on. But I think we're done with that for a while."

"So you'll become homebodies again?" said Harriet. "I liked it when you were a homebody, Odelia."

"Yeah, I kinda liked it, too," said Odelia with a smile. "And lucky for me Chase feels the same way."

"Chase feels the same way about what?" asked a voice behind her. Chase crouched down next to her and placed a hand on her back. "This is cozy."

"Hi, Chase," said Harriet coyly. She was a big fan of Chase, as were all of Odelia's cats, which was a good thing.

"They feel we've been neglecting them lately."

"Have we?"

"Yeah. We've been going out a lot, and they've missed spending time with us, huddling on the couch and watching silly shows and silly movies."

Chase gave Harriet a sheepish look. "Well, I guess you're right, Harriet. Odelia and I have spent a lot of time on the town. But that's all over now, isn't it, babe? We're ready to kick off our shoes and become Netflix nerds again."

"I like Netflix nerds," said Harriet.

"Me, too," said Brutus.

"And Max," said Odelia. "He loves being a couch potato even more than the rest of us. So where is he?"

Harriet and Brutus shared a look of concern. "I don't know," said Harriet. "I haven't seen him since we left him and Dooley at Chateau Leonidas."

"You mean they're still there?" said Odelia, concern lacing her voice.

"Who's still where?" asked Chase.

"Max and Dooley are still at the Flake place."

"What are they doing—oh, right. Interviewing pet witnesses, huh?"

"I hope so," said Odelia. Though it wasn't like Max not to come home after a day well spent hunting down clues and talking to pet witnesses. "Maybe we should go and look for them."

"I'm sure they're fine," said Chase, who had a lot of confidence in her cats' ability to take care of themselves.

"I'm not so sure," said Brutus. "He was pretty adamant about our strike."

"The strike? Oh, right, the strike."

"Yeah, he really ran with it. Said he would never help you investigate a crime ever again."

"Oh, dear," said Odelia.

CHAPTER 15

*U*nbeknownst to Odelia and Chase, or Harriet and Brutus, for that matter, their conversation hadn't remained as private as they would have liked it to be. Behind the backyard was a patch of fallow land where no house had been built yet. It was generally used by neighborhood kids to play on, or sometimes by a local farmer to put his sheep, and save the owner the trouble of taking out his lawnmower. It had been a while since the sheep had grazed there, though, and so the grass was high—so high that two people could easily hide in there, and aim a camera and a microphone at the backyard of the unsuspecting Odelia Poole and her future husband and their cats. And by the time Odelia and Chase returned indoors, Lauren Klepfisch patted Zak Kowalski on the back and said, "Did you get all that?"

"Yeah, sure, but I'm not sure what it is I got."

"Proof that Odelia Poole talks to her pets," said Lauren triumphantly.

"So? Plenty of people talk to their pets. My mom talks to her Chihuahua."

"Yeah, lots of people talk to their pets, but few people have their pets talk back to them, and are able to understand what they say."

"And you think that's what happened here?"

"Pretty sure it did. I'm not sure how it all works, but it was clear to me they were holding an entire conversation, and now we have everything on tape."

"So? What does it prove? That Odelia Poole is a little nutty?"

"That's for our viewers to decide. And I'm sure we'll get great coverage."

Zak got up and stretched his sore limbs. "I'm starting to understand what being a war correspondent feels like. Tough to have to lie in bushes."

"This is not war reporting, you idiot," Lauren snapped as she plucked a beetle from her shoulder. "For one thing, there are no snipers trying to kill us."

"Except for my colleague," he muttered darkly.

"So what did you think of Gabriel Crier? Do you think he did it?"

"How should I know? I'm not a cop," the cameraman grumbled as he swiped at the knees of his jeans where two nice patches of green had appeared.

"I think he did it," she said. "And a great story it is, too: Gay Lover Murders King Of Couture. It's the Gianni Versace thing all over again. Right here in the heart of the Hamptons. Oh, this is going to be a smash. My big break. And then the Odelia Poole pet whisperer thing on top of that, it's going to be the one-two punch that's going to blow all my competition out of the water!"

*C*hristopher Cross, the pet detective, was at that moment applying a slender finger to the buzzer of Chateau Leonidas and patiently waiting for the gates to swing open, which after a brief delay they did. He got back into the van and directed his vehicle along the long drive, his trusty feline sidekick next to him in the passenger seat.

"I wonder what she wants from us this time," grumbled Tank.

"Probably to hand us our paycheck," said Chris. "We cracked the case, didn't we? So time to pay up."

"We didn't crack the case, Chris," said the Siamese cat tersely. "The case cracked itself. Or should I say, Gabe cracked under the pressure and killed his lover."

"The operative word being cracked. The killer was caught so we need to get paid. It's as simple as that."

"Yeah, though I'm not so sure."

"Not so sure about what?"

"That they got the right guy!"

"He was caught red-handed. Why wouldn't he be the right guy?"

"'Cause those two idiots Max and Dooley are still hanging around the chateau, making nice with Flake's flock of barnyard animals. And let me ask you this: would they bother if the case was cracked? Let me answer that for you: no, they wouldn't!"

"Max and Dooley are idiots. They wouldn't know how to find a clue if it stared them right in the face."

"They may be idiots, but they still manage to solve a lot of cases, bud, or haven't you been reading dear Odelia Poole's articles?"

Chris had. In fact those articles were what had put him on this career path in the first place. He'd always had the knack of being able to communicate with his pets, even from a young age. And it had taken him a while to understand how unique this gift was. The truth had probably only dawned on him when his folks had sent him to his first shrink. Dr. Jinx had found nothing particularly wrong with him, apart from a childish belief he could talk to animals, which he described as the Dr. Dolittle Complex, a rare disease for which there was, alas, no cure. The advice Dr. Jinx had given Chris's parents was to simply ignore the affliction, and it would go away all by itself as he got older.

It hadn't gone away, but Chris had become hip to the fact that he was always going to be considered a weirdo if he kept insisting he could talk to animals, so from one day to the next he'd simply stopped mentioning the strange gift he had and that had elicited twin sighs of relief from his parents, not to mention the rest of his family. The revelation had come to him when Bethany Kernick, who was in his class, had told him he was a weirdo. Since he was deeply, madly in love with young Bethany at the time, he'd decided then and there that talking to animals was probably not the babe magnet he'd thought it was, and had decided to stop mentioning it to anyone. He'd even gone so far as to admit to Bethany that the only reason he'd told her he could talk to her pet hamster was to make an impression on her because he liked her so much. It had worked, and he and Bethany had gone steady for the rest of the semester, until she met Ernesto Hair and had declared him her boyfriend. It had been a valuable lesson for young Chris, though: don't let the world know that you're different, for it can only result in being bullied, or in girls like Bethany Kernick spurning your well-intentioned advances.

It had taken him well into his adult life to embrace his gift. Only when the rumor had reached his ear that Odelia Poole, of *Hampton Cove Gazette* fame, got a little help from her cats when researching her articles, did he finally realize his was a marketable trait, and so he'd gotten his PI license, hung out his shingle, and hadn't looked back since.

"So you think there's more to this story than meets the eye?" asked Chris.

"Oh, I'm pretty sure there is," said Tank in that gruff voice of his.

For a detective's pet sidekick Tank was a little on the belligerent side, but Chris didn't mind. As long as they got the job done, that's what counted.

"So let's poke around some more," he said. "Have you talked to Pussy?"

"Nah. Haven't been able to track her down."

"Talk to her. If anyone knows what's going on it's her. Spread some of that charm of yours. Put your winning personality on display."

"Yeah, yeah, yeah," Tank grumbled.

"Just... be nice, okay?"

"I'm always nice!"

"You weren't very nice to Max."

"Max is a fat dumbbell," said Tank, narrowing his eyes at the recollection.

"He's also the main competition. And if we're going to wipe out the competition, we'll have to be smart about it."

And then once Odelia Poole and Max were out of the picture, the world was their oyster. There was no limit to the heights they could rise as the only man-and-cat detective combo in the business, and soon the money would start rolling in like nobody's business. In fact he couldn't understand how Odelia Poole hadn't tapped the mother lode yet. Probably too dumb to understand that a private sleuth who could talk to animals was the cat's meow. Soon they'd be making Uncle Scrooge money, and the Bethany Kernicks of this world would weep bitter tears for turning him down for an Ernesto Hair.

Vengeance was his—and would be even sweeter than he'd imagined.

But first they needed to get rid of Odelia Poole and her dumb chums.

CHAPTER 16

*T*he meeting was about to commence, and Dooley and I were ready to attend and take copious notes so our friend behind the curtain would know what had been discussed in regards to her future fate.

People had been arriving in droves, chauffeured in by fancy cars, as we had been able to witness from our vantage point behind the second-floor window, and judging from the buzz downstairs things were hotting up quickly.

Pussy had already shown us the setup so we could follow the meeting as if seated on the first row. It was a room only Pussy appeared to have access to. Off Flake's bedroom, she simply put her paw against a hidden security pad, a section of the wall slid open, and we found ourselves in a secret room!

"Wow—real James Bond type of stuff," said Dooley.

Inside, a wall-to-wall row of screens showed us every part of the house. Apparently Flake had installed it a long time ago, as a parallel system to the official security setup. It was a fairly small space, and probably had to be, or else people would notice this architectural funny business. The state-of-the-art surveillance equipment could take a peek inside every corner of the chateau. Flake had cameras in every room, even the bathrooms, and according to Pussy the designer had spent hours in there, spying on guests and associates.

He liked to organize weekend getaways for the company's upper crust, and spy on them while they held secret meetings in their rooms, gossiping about Flake, or plotting against him. Many an executive had been given the boot after such a weekend, for scheming against the boss. It had been a way for the designer to keep his fingers in every possible pie, and hold the company reins firmly in hand. According to Pussy all of his other houses were equipped with the same setup, and even the company headquarters in Paris.

With another flick of the paw, Pussy booted up the system, and all the screens flickered to life—in black and white, of course. She handled the joystick with remarkable ease, and brought up one screen in particular: the main meeting room in the basement, where the conference was about to begin.

She flicked a button and now we had sound, too. She hopped down from the console and moved swiftly to the door. "Watch and learn, you guys."

"Maybe you should stay," I suggested.

"I told you, Max—I can't," she said, with the same pained look she'd displayed before. The loss of her human had hit her hard, that much was obvious, but the uncertainty about her future was even harder to bear.

"We'll tell you everything you need to know," Dooley promised.

She smiled. "You're good cats, both of you. Never change, will you?" And with these words she left the room, and allowed the hidden panel to swing back into place. Now we were effectively cut off from the rest of the house.

"Never change?" said Dooley. "What does she mean, Max?"

"I have no idea," I said, jumping up onto Flake's chair—the one where he spent all those hours spying on his own people —hunting down the plotters.

"Because we do change, don't we? I noticed this morning that a black hair is growing out of my left ear. And I'm pretty sure it wasn't there yesterday."

"A lot of hair grows out of your ears, Dooley. It's because you're a cat."

"Yeah, but like I said, this particular hair wasn't there before. And I know this because it's black, and I don't have black hairs growing out of my ears."

I wasn't going to discuss the color of the hairs in Dooley's ears, for judging from the buzz sounding from the speakers, the meeting was about to start. And since I didn't want to miss a thing—for Pussy's sake—focus was key.

"I could always pull out the hair, of course," Dooley went on. "But I'm not sure if that's the way to go. They do say that when you pull out a hair it only grows back thicker and more horrible than before. Or I could cut it. Maybe cutting a hair doesn't alter its shape and thickness? What do you think, Max?"

"I think I don't really care about a single hair in those hairy ears of yours, Dooley," I said as I watched the screen intently.

"Ouch. That's a mean thing to say, Max."

"It's one hair! Who cares?!"

"Well, I care. If hairs are going to start growing indiscriminately without my permission, what's next? I might turn into the hairiest cat alive if this keeps up."

"Lady cats love hair on a male cat," I said, in a bid to get him to shut up.

"They do? I didn't know that," he said, perking up.

"Oh, yeah. The hairier the merrier. Mark my words, the more hair you grow, the more attention you'll start getting from the ladies."

"Oh," he said. "I never looked at it that way."

He lapsed into silence, and I got ready to learn what I could about Pussy's fate. Then, suddenly, from the corner of my eye, I saw that Dooley was performing a peculiar ritual. I turned to him, and saw he was biting himself!

"Dooley! What are you doing?"

"I'm trying to pull out more hair," he said between two nips into his fur.

"But why?"

"You said it yourself, Max. The hairier the merrier. So I figure if I pull out all of my hair, it will only grow back thicker and shinier, and it will increase my appeal with a factor of at least twelve."

"Dooley, that whole spiel about hair growing back thicker is only a myth. It grows back, but not thicker than before."

"It doesn't?" he said, a tuft of gray hair between his lips.

"It doesn't. So please stop pulling out your hair and start watching the meeting with me, will you? We owe it to Pussy to do this right."

"Okay," he said, and spat out his hair, which fluttered to the concrete floor of Flake's secret control room.

On the screen, about a dozen people had taken a seat around the table. At the head of the table an old woman sat, and when I say old I mean ancient. She looked about a hundred, was seated in a wheelchair, and was sucking from an oxygen mask. Behind her stood a sturdy female nurse, administering the oxygen from a bulky tank on wheels.

For the rest there were plenty of men and women in suits, and they all looked very serious and businesslike.

"First off, I think I speak for all of us when I say we're all deeply shocked and saddened by the tragic death of our friend and founder, Leonidas Flake," suddenly spoke a man with a natty little mustache and thick-rimmed glasses. He was dressed in a charcoal suit, and his hair was combed neatly back from a high forehead. He now raised a glass of what looked like champagne. "A toast. To the man. The myth. The legend. *Monsieur* Leonidas Flake."

Echoes of his words rang out around the table, all those present standing for a moment—except the lady in the wheelchair—and raising their glasses in a salute to Leo Flake.

"I call this meeting to order," said the chairman. "And I think I speak for all of us when I say that the tragic events have shaken us to the core. Leo's death came as a shock to me personally, but I think it's imperative that we carry on. Leo would have wanted the company that he built from scratch to continue and to flourish, even without him."

"Is it true, Xavier, that Gabe is the culprit?" asked a woman with wavy blond hair.

"It would appear so," said Xavier, adjusting his glasses. "At least that's what the police have told me. Gabe has been arrested, and he has been charged."

Sounds of shock reverberated through the room.

"But why?" asked a well-coiffed older lady. "Why did he do it?"

"A lovers' tiff?" said Xavier, who seemed to be the one in charge. "A jealous rage? A momentary lapse of sanity? Who knows? I'm sure the police will keep us abreast of the exact circumstances of Leo's death. The only thing we need to concern ourselves with right now is the appointment of a new president and CEO and figuring out how to take this company into the future. Leonidas was a strong leader. A hands-on leader. And until the very last he designed all of his own collections, with the assistance of a small cadre of minions like myself," he added with a smile, "but always under his guiding genius. So the first question we need to ask ourselves is this: can we continue existing at the high level of excellence that we have, in the absence of the master couturier?"

For the next half hour or so, a discussion ensued on what, exactly, constituted the Leonidas Flake brand, and if it was possible for anyone to step into the shoes of the master, and provide continuity for a company now officially in crisis. Apparently in the recent past several talented designers had been hired to assist Flake, only to be kicked to the curb by the old master within the space of weeks or sometimes even days. It would appear he'd figured he'd live forever, and hadn't condoned anyone to take the baton.

The only one who'd come close was this Xavier person—full name Xavier Yesmanicki—who confessed he was more a glorified administrator than a creative genius like Leo Flake. At the end of the discussion, Xavier had assumed the role of president and CEO, and now the conversation turned to the recruitment of fresh talent, either in-house or outside the company, to create the spring collection—the fall collection had been created by Flake.

"This is not very interesting," said Dooley as the discussion flowed as easily as the champagne.

"No, it's not," I said. "And not a word about Pussy."

"I think they completely forgot about her."

"Yeah, just like Odelia has completely forgotten about us," I said with a touch of bitterness. Humans weren't as trustworthy as I'd always imagined. When push came to shove, they preferred to be surrounded by other humans, not the feline species they professed to love so much.

But then, suddenly, the old lady in the wheelchair piped up. She'd put down the oxygen mask and spoke with a croaky but clear voice.

"You're all nuts!" she declared, and silence immediately descended upon the room. "Don't you realize you're wasting your time? My son decided to leave his entire fortune, and the company he built, to a cat!"

"I don't think—" Xavier began with a little smile.

"A darn cat! Who cares who the new CEO or president is? From now on, Leo's cat is in charge! She's going to sign the paychecks. She's your boss!"

"But surely a cat can't run a business," said the well-coiffed woman.

"Yes, that is simply ludicrous!" said another.

"You're right! Cats don't run companies! So my son appointed a guardian for his cat, and so this guardian will effectively run things from now on."

"Who's the guardian?" asked one of the suits.

"And how do you know all this?" asked another.

"Because Leo's lawyer is also my lawyer. And the guy called me the minute he learned about what happened. So the lawyer told me about Leo's will—apparently he'd only had it drawn up last week—and the cat situation, and I was as shocked as you are. And as shocked as I'm sure the rest of the world will be when they find out about my son's final folly. They'll all be surprised to learn that Leo went a little cuckoo at the end. But the fact remains that Pussy now owns the company!"

"Can't this will be contested on account of the fact that the person who made it was... well, not to put too fine a point on it... nuts?" asked another suit.

Xavier spread his arms. "Leo wasn't nuts," he said. "Just... a little eccentric." He looked flustered. He probably hadn't expected to have to report to a cat from now on.

"Well, the lawyer assured me that Leo was of sound mind and body when he drew up his new will," said Leo's mother after taking a gasp from her oxygen tank. "And that it will stand the tests of the courts and whatever else you want to throw at it. The only problem is that the guardian is now in jail for murder, and won't be able to take up his role."

"The guardian is Gabriel Crier?" asked Xavier, looking flabbergasted.

"Yes, it is. And since he killed my son, and will be sent to Rikers Island if there's any justice in the world, the law clearly states that the next person in line for this guardianship is Leo's next of kin." She tapped her chest. "Moi."

CHAPTER 17

*T*he meeting turned into complete pandemonium. People were rocketing up out of their chairs, they were screaming, some were pulling at their hair, while others hammered the table with their fists, one even with his head.

"Silence!" suddenly a voice bellowed. It was hard to imagine, but it actually came from the old lady who looked a hundred, and who probably was a hundred, but who was as vivid and lively as any of her cronies.

"But this is an outrage!" Xavier was crying. "This will not stand!"

"Yes, how can a cat—a cat!—run this company!" someone else said, clearly speaking for all those present.

"I take offense, Max," said Dooley. "A cat can just as easily run a company as any human, right?"

"I would think so," I said. Though I had no personal experience running a company, I could well imagine that a cat, given the proper training, could run a company just as well as the next CEO. After all, a lot of Fortune 500 companies are run by jackals and hyenas, and some even by an ass.

"Pussy is quite capable of running this company," said Leo's mother, echoing our words exactly.

"I think I like this woman," said Dooley.

"A woman after my own heart," I agreed.

"At least she seems to appreciate that sometimes the smartest person in the room is a cat," said Dooley.

"But you don't even know what she thinks!" said Xavier, whose hair was now all mussed and whose glasses were bedewed with honest perspiration.

"I don't claim to understand cats either," said the old lady. "But fortunately I know someone who does. Come on in, Chris!" she yelled in that same hale and hearty voice of hers that resonated through the room—both the one in the basement and the one Dooley and I were currently holed up in.

Chris came in, and to my surprise it was the pet detective.

"Isn't that..." said Dooley.

"Yeah, I think it is," I said.

To remove the last vestige of doubt as to who he was, the Siamese cat that had been so rude to us walked right behind him, and immediately meowed, "What a bunch of losers, boss!"

"Yeah, I know," said his boss.

Lucky for him no one understood what they were saying, which seemed to add to their enjoyment, for they both smiled. Yes, cats do smile, even though there is some discussion about that. Some scientists claim they don't, while other, equally learned scholars claim that they do. Well, let me clear up this misunderstanding: we do smile, but since we have a very refined sense of humor, we rarely indulge in the habit, so you probably missed it that time.

"Gentlemen and ladies," said Leo's mother, "let me introduce you to Christopher Cross and his trusty sidekick Tank. Chris is a latter-day Dr. Dolittle, in the sense that he can talk to any pet, great or small, and can actually understand what those pets are talking about. He's the original pet whisperer, and I'm very grateful that he's accepted my invitation to play a senior role in the newly structured Leonidas Flake Company."

There was more shouting, this time directed at the newcomer, but the old lady once again managed to drown out the hubbub with her stentorian voice.

"This is how it's going to be from now on! Pussy will take on the role of company president, and her dictates will be carefully noted by Chris and Tank, then turned into instructions and executive orders, which will trickle down through the company. I will be on hand to keep an eye on the proceedings, as I have formed a close bond with Pussy myself, and will play a vital role in the new structure that will be put in place."

"But what role will you assume?" asked an exasperated chairman.

The lady puffed out her chest. "I'm the new CEO. And together with my president I will make this company great again!"

"This is an outrage!" someone yelled.

"Well, you don't have to feel that way anymore," said the woman, after taking a puff from her oxygen mask. "You're fired, effective immediately."

A collective gasp of shock reverberated through the room.

"Anyone else want to lodge a formal complaint about the new management structure?" asked Mrs. Flake.

"I don't want to sound critical…" the well-coiffed lady began.

"I have a feeling you will."

"But aren't you a little… old for the role, Mrs. Flake?"

"You're only as old as you feel," said Leo's mother. "And I feel a sprightly fifty, so I have a lot of good years still left in the tank." She patted the oxygen tank for good measure. "Anyone else? Comments, criticisms? No? Then court is adjourned and I'll see you lot in Paris for our annual board meeting where we will formalize the new company structure and I hope to be able to convey to you some of the new plans I'm sure Pussy will be excited to come up with."

"Oh, boy," I said. "Pussy isn't going to like this."

"Why not?" said Dooley. "She's president of the company now."

"I'm not sure that's what she wants, though."

Pussy, who had an impeccable sense of timing, chose that moment to join us again. "Is the meeting over?"

"Yeah, it's over," I said, gesturing to the screen, where people were now shouting and screaming and all hell seemed to have broken loose.

"What's going on?" asked Pussy with a frown. "Are they fighting?"

"Pretty much."

"You're in charge now, Pussy," said Dooley, clapping his paws with glee. "From now on you are the president of the Leonidas Flake Company!"

"Come again?" said Pussy after a pause. "I'm what now?"

"You're in charge," I said. "Leo's mother took over the meeting and announced that you're the new president. It's official."

"But... I can't run a company," said Pussy, looking seriously distraught.

"I'm sure Mrs. Flake will help you with the finer points of running the business. She'll be your CEO so she'll be in charge of the day-to-day stuff."

"But I don't know the first thing about fashion!"

"You could have fooled me," I said, indicating the crown and the pendant she was still rocking.

"Oh, that," she said modestly. "Just something I threw on this morning. No, but seriously, what did they say?"

"Exactly that. They've appointed a pet whisperer, some guy named Christopher Cross, to be your official translator, along with his cat Tank."

"Not a very nice cat," said Dooley.

"Not a very nice cat," I agreed. "But maybe he'll grow on you as you take the reins."

"So some guy is going to sit in my office and translate my decisions to the CEO, who will be Leo's mother?"

"That seems to be the gist."

"But… Leo didn't even like his mother. In fact it's safe to say he hated her."

"He did? Odd."

"Not so odd. The woman is crazy. Power hungry and mad. Leonora always felt Leo should have given her a bigger stake in the company, and when Leo refused, she went bananas. She tried to get him removed from his own company by bribing several board members to get him kicked out for mental health reasons, and when that didn't work she joined forces with LMVH, a large luxury goods conglomerate, to organize a hostile takeover of the company, forcing Leo out. That didn't work either, but it caused Leo a big headache for a while."

"That must have been tough," I said sympathetically.

"It was especially tough on Gabe. They never used to fight like they fought these last couple of months."

"So is that what they fought about?"

"Gabe felt Leo worked too hard, and wanted him to slow down, and even thought that this takeover was a good thing. These LMVH people know their stuff, so the future of the Leonidas Flake brand was safe, and the takeover would make Leo a very rich man. But Leo felt that Gabe didn't understand. He couldn't lose control over his company. It was, after all, his life's work. And so they fought a lot."

"And then last night Gabe snapped and killed him."

"Is that the official story?"

"Yeah, that seems to be the way it went down."

"I'm sorry to say I wasn't there," she said softly. "When Leo was murdered I was holed up in my room. I never liked it when they fought, so I got out of there the moment the shouting began. If only I'd been there…"

"You can't think like that," said Dooley immediately.

She nodded. "It's hard to imagine Gabe would do such a horrible thing. Those two loved each other so, so much. You should have seen them together. They were crazy about each other. Even now, after all these years."

"Well, what happened, happened," I said. "And now you're the boss, and you can do whatever you want."

"But I don't want to be the boss," said Pussy stubbornly. "I want Leo back, and Gabe, and the three of us on the couch watching *Project Runway* or *RuPaul's Drag Race*."

"We used to watch a lot of TV with Odelia, too," I said wistfully. "Only now she's too busy to bother."

"Good times," Dooley murmured.

"You'll do great," I told the gorgeous feline. "You'll do Leo proud."

In response, Pussy merely groaned. Obviously she wasn't so sure.

We heard voices, and with a flick of the wrist Pussy flipped through several screens until she'd called up the one where the voices were coming from: we saw Leonora Flake, along with her nurse, Christopher Cross and Tank step into Pussy's room.

"Uh-oh," said Pussy. "I think they're looking for me."

"Well, better put in an appearance," I said. "Or else they'll organize a search party. You are, after all, the new company president."

The three of us quickly moved through the hidden panel and into Leo's bedroom, then via the corridor to Pussy's very own domain, where we were greeted by a small welcoming committee.

"What's all this?" asked Leonora Flake. "I thought my son only had one cat?"

"That's Max and Dooley," Chris Cross said. "They belong to Odelia Poole, a local nosy parker."

"Oh, right," said Leonora. "She was snooping around here this morning, wasn't she? Assisting the cops."

"She was, and she seems to have left her feline brood behind to keep an eye on things."

"I told you to take a hike, didn't I?" growled Tank.

"You're not the boss of us," said Dooley, quite sensibly, I thought.

"What are they saying?" asked Mrs. Flake.

"That we're not the boss of them," said Chris.

It surprised me greatly to meet another human who could understand what we said, but the surprise was short-lived, for Leonora laughed loudly and said, "Clever little pussies." Then the smile disappeared. "Get rid of them, will you? We don't need a bunch of annoying busybodies."

Chris took one step in our direction, but Pussy said, "They're staying put!"

Chris frowned at the cat. "You can't be serious."

"What's going on?" asked Leonora, who was starting to resemble a cuckoo clock.

"Pussy wants those two to stick around."

"Oh, for crying out loud," she said. "Lock 'em up, will you? And make sure they stay out of sight."

"Will do," said Chris curtly, and the small band of humans left the room.

The last one to leave was Tank, and when he turned to us it was with a cruel grin on his face. "Told you," he said with a silky voice, then walked out.

"What's happening, Max?" asked Dooley.

"I have a feeling we're about to become like the man in the iron mask," I said.

"Leonardo DiCaprio?" asked Dooley, excitedly. Dooley knows his movies.

"Who's the man in the iron mask?" asked Pussy.

The door closed and a key was turned.

"Quick. Into the next room!" I said, and we sprinted for the door. Only to see it slammed shut in front of our faces, and locked from the outside.

"The man in the iron mask was a prisoner in the French Bastille—a famous former Paris prison," I told Pussy as I caught my breath. "He was forced to wear a mask—hence the moniker—so no one would know who he was. Rumor had it that he was the king's twin brother, and imprisoned in a dispute over the throne. In the movie version he was played by Leo DiCaprio."

"Leo loved Leo," said Pussy reverently. "And so do I."

"I love Leo, too," said Dooley. "Not your Leo, I mean, but-but-but…"

Pussy smiled. "I know what you mean, Dooley," she said.

Dooley blinked and I frowned. I'd never seen him this flustered before.

"So what happened to the man in the iron mask?" asked Pussy.

"Oh, he died in prison," I said.

"But he didn't die in the movie!" said Dooley, eyes widening. "He lived happily ever after!"

"That's Hollywood for you. Always going for the happy end."

"I think I like the Hollywood version better, Max!"

"Me, too, Dooley," I said. "But this isn't a movie, is it?"

"Oh, cheer up, you guys," said Pussy. "I'm the company president now, right? So they're not going to lock me up and throw away the key. Right?"

I didn't respond. Because I had a feeling that was exactly what they were going to do.

CHAPTER 18

*I*t was late by the time Odelia and Chase arrived at the chateau, but that didn't deter the intrepid reporter from pressing her finger to the bell and to keep on pressing until a gruff voice spoke through the intercom.

"What do you want?" the voiced inquired.

It was a far cry from the warm welcome they'd enjoyed that morning, but Odelia wasn't deterred. "Hi, My name is Odelia Poole, and I think my cats are somewhere on the premises. Do you mind if we take a look around?"

"Yes, I do mind," said the gruff voice. "This is a private residence and you can't just barge in here without an appointment. Now please go away."

Next it was Chase's turn to press his finger to the bell.

"I told you to leave!" the voice growled when it returned.

Chase held his police badge in front of the camera. "Chase Kingsley, Detective with the Hampton Cove Police Department. Open the gate."

"That badge doesn't give you the right to snoop around, Detective. I suggest you come back with a warrant. Until you

126

do, get lost." And the connection was once again abruptly severed.

Odelia stared at the gate for a moment. She couldn't believe what was happening. "Did they really just tell us to take a hike?"

"I guess they did," said Chase, who looked as surprised as Odelia.

Just then, the gate swung open, and moments later a small fleet of black SUVs exited. They all seemed to be in a hurry to get away from the place.

"Huh," said Odelia. "I didn't know there was a UN meeting taking place."

"Time to go look for your cats," said Chase, and walked through the gate, Odelia close on his heels.

"Don't you think we'll get in trouble for this?" she asked.

"Pretty sure the gate swung open after we rang the bell."

She grinned. "Well, if you look at it that way, I guess you're right."

"Stick with me, kid," he quipped. "I'm always right."

"Big man on campus," she said as she had to hurry to keep up with the long-legged cop.

"So where did you last see your cats?" he asked.

"When we got here this morning, remember? They got out of the car and that's the last time I saw them."

"They could literally be anywhere. They could even be roaming the streets of Hampton Cove right now."

"They could," she agreed, "but something tells me they never left."

"Don't tell me. Female intuition?"

"You may scoff at the notion that women have a very powerful and fine-tuned sense of intuition, but it's a fact that very often we're right."

"I'm not making fun of you, babe. I do believe you when

you say your cats are here. No one else I know has such a strong connection to their pets."

"Thanks," she said. "That's a very nice thing to say."

They'd arrived at the house and now stood where their car had been parked that morning: in the drive in front of the house.

All the lights were out inside, except on the second floor.

"Why don't we knock on the door and go in?" Chase suggested. "After all, we're still laboring under the assumption we were buzzed in just now."

"A false assumption," she reminded him.

"Yeah, but they don't know that we know that."

So they moved up to the house and Chase pounded his fist on the door. Of course there was no response.

"Let's move to the back," said Odelia. "Maybe Max and Dooley are still around somewhere."

They walked around to the back of the house, and in the distance Odelia could see the famous petting zoo. The lights were on in the different sections and she could see a horse staring back at her, and also a donkey.

"You can't talk to them, can you?" asked Chase.

"No, unfortunately I can only talk to cats."

"Too bad. They might know where Max and Dooley went."

And they'd reached the deck when suddenly floodlights bathed the scene in a blinding light. Moments later they were surrounded by a small group of armed men, whom Odelia recognized as part of the house's security detail.

"Easy, guys," said Chase, carefully taking out his police badge. "We were invited."

"Oh, hey, Detective Kingsley," said the burliest and biggest of the lot. "Going for an evening stroll?"

"Yeah, enjoying the night air," he said. "So what's going on here? What's with all the SUVs that just drove off?"

"Oh, we had a conference of some kind," said the guy, who appeared to be the more garrulous type. With a gesture of the hand he dismissed his men, who holstered their weapons and returned indoors, to fight off another threat to the safety of the chateau's inhabitants.

"A conference?" asked Odelia.

"Yeah. Discussing the future of the company now that the top guy is dead."

"So who's the new top guy?" asked Chase.

"I'm not sure but I think it's Leonora Flake," said the guy. "At least that's who we're getting our instructions from now. Her and some skinny dude with a cat."

"Skinny dude with a cat?" asked Chase.

"Not Chris Cross," said Odelia, surprised.

"Yeah, Cross. That's the name I got."

"Is he in charge now? I thought he was just a private detective, hired by Leonora?"

"Yeah, well, I guess he got promoted."

"Weird," said Chase.

"So have you seen any other cats around? "asked Odelia. "My cats in particular? One is large and orange, the other small and gray."

The guy furrowed his brow. "Um… can't say that I have, Miss…"

"Poole."

"Oh, right. I've read your articles, Miss Poole. Well-written and well-informed every time. They're the first thing I read when I get the *Gazette*."

"Thanks," said Odelia. "Always nice to meet a fan. So no cats, huh?"

"Only Pussy, but then she's the star of the show, isn't she?" said the guy with a laugh. He turned to Chase. "So did you arrest Gabe Crier?"

"Yeah, we did. And charged him."

"Yeah, seems like a foregone conclusion that he did it. Martha is still pretty shook up. And now even more, since she got fired."

"Who's Martha?" asked Odelia.

"The maid who discovered the body," said Chase. "She got fired?"

"Yeah, her and all the others. Looks like Leonora is doing a clean sweep. The entire household staff was fired this evening, and sent home. Tomorrow she'll start hiring new people. At least security hasn't been given their marching orders yet, but I have a hunch we're next. New brooms, huh?"

And with these words he wandered back to the house and disappeared inside.

Odelia and Chase stared after the man. "What do you make of that?" asked Odelia. "Leonora in charge, with a pet detective and his cat, and the entire staff fired."

"Like the guy said. New brooms."

Odelia thought for a moment. "Maybe that's why they hired Chris Cross. He claims to be able to talk to pets, just like me. Only I always thought it was just a gimmick. You know, like a sales pitch."

"Maybe he really can talk to pets, and now he'll talk to Pussy and together they'll run the show."

Odelia glanced around. They still had no clue where Max and Dooley could be, and she was seriously starting to get worried now.

Chase, who could sense her agitation, said, "They're probably home by now. Strike or no strike, they don't like to be out and about for too long."

"No, they don't," she agreed. "Maybe it's time for us to head back."

And so they strolled back to the front of the house.

. . .

*A*bove their heads, and unbeknownst to them, three cats were yelling their little hearts out, pounding the window of Pussy's room. Unfortunately a cat's paws are outfitted with soft pink pads, and soft pink pads are not what you want when you try to attract attention by pounding on windows. The upshot was that their efforts produced no effect. And so it was with a desperate eye that Max and Dooley and Pussy saw the two humans who could have saved them from their imprisonment walk away and pass into the night.

CHAPTER 19

"*H*ow can they not have seen us?" asked Dooley with asperity.

"I guess they didn't," I said, feeling extremely disappointed in my human. I'd always assumed that Odelia and I shared a sacred bond. The kind of bond whereby she would instinctively know I was in grave danger and she'd come running to offer aid and support no matter the obstacles in her path. But whatever bond we'd once shared was clearly in very bad shape indeed, for even though I'd willed her to look up, she hadn't done so once. Not a glimpse.

"Maybe they're simply pretending not to notice us to throw Leonora and Chris Cross and Tank off the scent," said Dooley, cheering up. "And any moment now they'll come barging in here with the entire Hampton Cove police force and save us!"

"I don't think, so, Dooley. They simply didn't see us."

"But how is that possible? It's Odelia. She has to see us. She's our human."

"I'm starting to think she no longer is," I said.

And we would have discussed the topic in depth if the

door hadn't swung open at that exact moment and the same motley crew that had locked us up was upon us once more: Leonora Flake, pushed by her strangely stoic nurse, Chris Cross and his feline sidekick Tank.

"Keep an eye on them, Tank," said Chris. "Those two are cunning."

"They don't look cunning," said Tank. "In fact they look pretty dumb. Dumb and dumber." He laughed at his own joke, and so did Chris Cross.

"Will you stop with the inside jokes already?" said Leonora irritably. "So have we decided? Out with the intruders and in with Little Miss Sweet?"

"Yeah, I guess that's the only way to go," said Chris. "Max and Dooley clearly know too much now, and the moment we set them loose they'll run and tell mama. And we can't do without Pussy, in case we need to show her to the investors or the board at some point."

"Fine. Do it quietly, though, will you? And make sure no one sees you."

"Wait, you expect *me* to do it? Why don't you do it?"

"Have you seen the wheelchair?"

"I wasn't talking about you. I was talking about Nurse Ratched over there."

Nurse Ratched didn't seem all that happy with her new moniker. "My name is Helga Cooper," she said in clipped tones. "And nowhere does it say in my job description that I should go around murdering cats. So I refuse."

"You do it," Leonora told Chris. "You're good with cats."

"I'm good with live cats, not dead ones!"

"Oh, for crying out loud!"

Dooley, who'd been gulping freely next to me, appeared on the verge of a panic attack. "They're going to kill us, Max!" he cried. "Did you hear that? They're going to kill us and throw away the bodies!"

"Bury the bodies, most likely," said Tank with an evil glint in his eyes. "Deep, so that no one will ever find you. And if by some miracle they do, the worms will have eaten through your rotting corpses and all that will be left will be your bones. Sad, sad bones."

"Oh, no!" said Dooley, hyperventilating now.

"Deep breaths, Dooley," I said. "Deep, steady breaths."

"Look, you don't have to do this," said Pussy. "You can keep us all in here and no one has to die."

"Yeah, I know we don't *have* to do it," said Tank. "But that's just the thing: we want to do it." He turned to Chris. "Let me do it, boss."

"You? You can't kill those two."

"Oh, but I can," said Tank, licking his lips and extending a gleaming claw. "In fact I know just how. One nice jab to the jugular and they'll bleed out like gutted pigs. And then all you have to do is dig the hole and dump the bodies."

"I don't want to die, Max!" Dooley cried. "I'm too young to die!"

"I don't want to die either, Dooley," I said, and already I was eyeing the door with a keen eye. "If we move fast," I whispered in his ear, "we can make it. On three. One two three—go!"

And I raced for the door. Only I felt a keen sense of emptiness behind me and when I looked back I saw that Dooley was glued to the spot, looking at me with wide panicky eyes. So I halted and retraced my steps.

"Ha ha ha!" Tank laughed. "Look at them. Dumb and dumber—the sequel!"

"Close the door, you idiots," Leonora snapped. "If they get out they'll spill the beans and then all this will have been for naught."

"Max," said Dooley when I'd returned to his side. "Why didn't you make a run for it?"

"I couldn't very well leave my best friend behind, could I?"

"But you could have escaped and warned Odelia!"

Oh, shoot. Why hadn't I thought of that!

"So this is your final word?" asked Leonora.

"This is my final word," Chris confirmed. "I'm not a cat killer. If you want them dead, you'll have to find someone else to do it."

"Imbeciles and incompetents!" shouted Leonora as she directed her wheelchair to the door. "I'm surrounded by imbeciles and incompetents!" She passed through the door, followed by Helga and Chris. The last one to leave us in our new prison was, of course, Tank.

"Too bad they didn't task me with the kill," he said. And he slashed the air with his gleaming claw. Then the door closed and we were once again alone.

"Someone will come for us," said Pussy. "Your humans will realize what's going on and they'll come looking for you."

Under normal circumstances I would have heartily agreed with her. Only this time I had the distinct impression that no one would come for us. Or even if they did, it would be too late, and we'd already be dead and buried.

CHAPTER 20

*G*ran wasn't feeling like herself. Ever since her granddaughter had branched out into the world of private detecting, she'd been her loyal and able sidekick on many an investigation. Today, though, things hadn't gone according to plan, to say the least. The worst kind of investigation was the one that was over before it even got started. And yet...

While at the reception desk in her son-in-law's office, she'd been surfing the web on the newly minted smartphone Tex had gifted her, and she discovered a couple of things about the case that greatly worried her. For one thing, by all accounts Leonidas Flake and Gabriel Crier had been a devoted couple. They'd been together for thirty years, and all that time they'd appeared in public displaying an affection that was unmistakable. It was hard to imagine that suddenly one partner in the tryst would snap and murder the other partner in the tryst and then not even remember what he'd done.

Furthermore, there had been rumors that the empire Leo had built was rocking on its foundations, not least because his mother was shaking the tree, insisting her son was squandering his legacy by bad business decisions. The woman had actually had the gall to try and oust her son from his own company by launching a hostile takeover bid. The fact that it had failed didn't mean much in the grand scheme of things. It had spooked investors, and the stock had been trading at an all-time low.

Shops had been closed, sales had slumped, and the company was on shaky ground. And now this murder. Gran couldn't help but feel there was more to the murder than a simple lovers' tiff. Rumors had been flying around all day that now that her son was dead, Mama Flake was moving in and finalizing her takeover attempt. She'd been spotted in town, even before the murder, staying at the Hampton Cove Star, which was highly suspect to say the least. Then again, Ma Flake was old. She was ninety-eight, and wheelchair bound, so it was hardly feasible she would have held the knife that killed her only son.

Furthermore, after the bad blood that had existed between herself and her son, she'd become persona non grata at Chateau Leonidas and hadn't been allowed to set foot inside the premises. At least not until today. So even if she'd wanted to murder her son, she wouldn't have had the chance.

Still, Gran felt there were loose ends attached to this case, and had already placed a strongly worded phone call to her own son Alec, telling him not to put all his eggs in one basket but to give the investigation another chance.

So great was her concern that when she arrived home after her shift, instead of plunking down in front of the TV to watch *Jeopardy!*, she hunkered down at the kitchen table to do some more digging into the family Flake.

Her daughter Marge, when arriving home from the library, watched her with a curious eye. "What's going on with you, Ma? No *Jeopardy!* today?"

"Murder investigation," she grunted curtly.

"Not the Flake case? Terrible business, that. I loved the man's designs."

This had Gran look up in surprise. "You liked Flake's designs?"

"Yeah, loved them. I have several Leonidas Flakes upstairs. Of course I only wear them on special occasions."

"What's this about special occasions, hon?" asked Tex, coming into the kitchen to grab something from the fridge.

"Leonidas Flake. Remember him?"

"Oh, of course. Terrible business. I have several Flake suits upstairs."

"You have Flake suits?" asked Gran. "But they cost a fortune."

"Oh, no," said Marge. "He has his haute couture line, of course, and those pieces are priceless, but he has his prêt-à-porter line and he did a collaboration with the Gap a couple of years ago, and those were very reasonably priced."

"Very reasonably priced," Tex agreed as he took a barbe-cued chicken wing from the fridge and gave it a tentative nibble.

"Leonidas Flake and the Gap? Well, what do you know?" said Gran.

"Lots of designers pull stunts like that," said Marge. "Stella McCartney did a line for H&M a couple of years ago, and I heard Vera Wang might team up with Costco next year. If they want to survive, these high-end fashion brands need to find a fresh clientele. They can't go on like they used to, and only sell the high-priced stuff in their flagship stores on Fifth Avenue or whatever. It's called the democratization of fashion and Leonidas Flake was all for it."

"The opportunity for the common man and woman to wear haute couture is a chance you don't want to miss, Vesta," said Tex, waving the chicken wing.

Gran felt like grabbing the chicken wing and shoving it down Tex's throat, but she restrained herself with a powerful effort. For some reason her son-in-law always brought out the worst in her, even though by all accounts he was a great guy, and she couldn't have wished Marge a better husband.

"I've been looking into this Flake," she said, "and all his business decisions the last couple of years have been sound. Extremely sound, in fact. His worst period seems to have been the early eighties, when he was on the verge of collapse. The big turnaround for him came about thirty years ago—not coincidentally the year he met Gabriel Crier."

"Leo Flake always called Gabe Crier his good-luck charm," said Marge.

Gran goggled at her daughter. "How come you know so much about Flake? I never even heard of the guy before today."

Marge shrugged. "I guess I like to read about fashion," she said, suddenly displaying a slight blush.

"Your daughter has quite the passion for fashion," Tex quipped. "In fact if she hadn't found a job at the library she would have gone into designing, isn't that right, darling?"

"Yeah, well, I guess it's a little hobby of mine," said Marge. "And I wouldn't mind designing a few pieces from time to time."

"Well, why don't you?" said Tex. "You never know where it will take you."

"Oh, but I'm not a designer, darling."

"I'm not saying you are and I'm not saying you aren't. I'm just saying give it a shot."

"Oh, darling," said Marge, and wrapped her arms around her husband's neck. "Look at you being all supportive."

"That's because I love you, my sweet, and I want you to be happy."

Kissing ensued, and Gran rolled her eyes. "So this Gabriel

guy is the real genius behind Flake's success?" she asked, trying to get the lovebirds back on track.

"Well, no, the real genius has always been Leo Flake," said Marge. "But even a genius can have a lesser period. And that lesser period threatened to derail his career, until he met Gabe, and that's when the magic returned."

"Huh," said Gran. "Interesting. So by all rights Gabe should be the one to take over the company now that his boyfriend is dead."

"Yeah, but that will never happen," said Tex. "Because Gabe is a murderer. And murderers don't run companies, do they?" He was talking to Gran as if she were a toddler, and she had to bite back a scathing retort or two.

"Yeah, tough to run a company from prison," she said.

"Too bad," said Marge. "With Leonora in charge things don't look too good. She's very old-fashioned, and has been dying to return to the old way of doing business: only high-end fashion and only selling through a few well-chosen flagship stores. So no more Leonidas Flake for me, I'm afraid."

"Design your own dresses, darling," said Tex. "And a few tuxes for me, while you're at it."

"Oh, I couldn't," said Marge.

"No, I'm telling you you could."

"Oh, darling, no."

"Yes, darling, yes."

"Oh, for crying out loud," Gran groaned, and took her phone and walked out of the house, through the backyard, through the hole in the hedge, into Odelia's backyard, and then into the house through the sliding glass door.

She plunked herself down at the kitchen table and was gratified to find that Odelia was out so she had the place to herself. Sometimes that was exactly what a person needed: some peace and quiet to hear oneself think.

And she'd been sitting there for a couple of minutes, her

Wi-Fi switched over to Odelia's network, when Harriet hopped up onto the high stool next to hers and gave her a plaintive look.

"Gran," she said. "Have you seen Max and Dooley?"

"No, I haven't," said Gran. "Why? Are they missing?"

"I guess they are," said Harriet. "First they went on strike, and then they disappeared."

"They should have been home by now," grumbled Brutus, taking up position on the stool to Gran's other side.

"They're probably in town or in the park," said Gran distractedly while she read through Gabe Crier's Wikipedia page again.

"I guess they are," said Harriet dubiously.

It was actually the first time that Harriet had expressed concern about Max, and the realization made Gran sit up. "So what makes you think they're in trouble?"

"I'm not sure," said Harriet. "Just a bad feeling I have."

"Yeah, I have a bad feeling, too," said Brutus.

Huh. Two cats with bad feelings. That was a first. "What do you think happened?" she asked. Others might scoff at feline intuition, just as they might scoff at female intuition, but Gran, after a long life lived in the company of cats, knew never to discard those sensations. Often they were warranted.

"I'm not sure," said Harriet. "But they should be home by now."

"Yeah, Max isn't one to miss his dinner," said Brutus.

"Nor is Dooley," Harriet added.

"We told Odelia and Chase, and they left to look for them," said Brutus.

"Oh, so Odelia is on the case? Then you've got nothing to worry about. If anyone can find them it's Odelia. She and Max share a special bond."

"Not lately," said Harriet.

"What do you mean?"

"Odelia has been neglecting us. Which is why we went on strike."

"You went on strike?" asked Gran with a laugh.

"Yeah, all of us," said Brutus. "If Odelia stops sending the love, we stop helping her catch the bad guys or write her articles. So we went on strike."

"Huh," said Gran. It made perfect sense to her. If Odelia decided to ignore her precious cats, of course they would rebel. "You did the right thing," she said. "Though you might have talked to Odelia before you decided to go on strike. I mean, how do you know she knows you're on strike, if you know what I mean? And if she doesn't know, how can she be expected to change?"

This made both Harriet and Brutus think for a moment.

"Yeah, I guess we should have said something," Harriet finally admitted.

"We were upset," said Brutus. "So we didn't think."

"Don't worry. It's been known to happen to me," said Gran. "Now why don't we simply wait for Odelia to return? I'm sure she'll find Max and Dooley. Okay?"

Both cats nodded, clearly much relieved. It touched Gran's heart to know how much her cats cared for each other. Usually cats are characterized as solitary creatures who don't play nice with other members of their species, but that obviously wasn't the case with Max, Dooley, Harriet and Brutus. They were a foursome that watched out for one another.

"What are you doing, Gran?" asked Harriet now, her most pressing concern addressed and alleviated.

"The Leonidas Flake business. I'm not so sure they got the right guy."

"You don't think the lover did it?" asked Brutus.

"Just a hunch," she said. "Like you with Max missing?

142

Same for me with this case. Just a hunch not all is as it seems."

"We should probably talk to Pussy," said Harriet.

"Pussy? I thought you had talked to her."

"No, we didn't," said Harriet. "We were on strike, remember?"

Harriet was right. If there was one cat who knew what was going on, it would be Pussy. And so Gran made one of those impulsive decisions that were typical of her and could drive the people around her up the wall sometimes. "Let's go," she told Harriet and Brutus, and jumped down from the stool.

"Go where?" asked Harriet, perking up.

"We're driving over to the Flake place to talk to Pussy. I don't know why, but I have a strong suspicion she's the key to this whole darn mystery."

CHAPTER 21

"*I* want you to know, Max," said Dooley, "that you've always been the cat in the world I've admired the most."

"Thanks, I guess," I said. I was pacing the room, trying to come up with a way out of our predicament. It was a little hard to see how, though, as the room had been designed to keep its inhabitants in, or at least that was my impression.

"And I want you to know that you can have all my earthly possessions after I'm gone," Dooley continued.

"You seem to forget that if you die, I'm dying along with you, Dooley."

This seemed to give him pause. "Oh, right," he said. "I forgot about that. So to whom can I dictate my last will and testament?" He turned to Pussy. "Pussy, I've always admired you from afar, and I want you to know—"

"You didn't even know me before today," said Pussy. "And besides, once you two are dead I might as well be dead, too. They're never going to let me out of this room. This is going to be my prison until the day I die, which might be sooner than I want. Cats in captivity rarely live to a ripe old age."

144

"How old are you now?" asked Dooley, interested.

"Four."

"Oh? You look a lot older."

"Um, thanks, I guess."

I'd already checked the windows, but they were all locked solid, the door was one of those rusty steel doors that Leo seemed to have favored, so no dice either, and there were no nooks and crannies that could assist us in our escape. Unless...

I glanced up and noticed that the ventilation system in the room was of an odd design. In line with the rest of the house it had an industrial look: the pipes led straight into the room and hung suspended from the ceiling with a series of rings and bolts and iron wiring. If only we could get up there, and pry loose one of those grates, we might have a shot at getting out of the room.

"No, really," Dooley was saying. "I thought you were six, or maybe seven."

"Uh-huh," said Pussy. "Is that a fact?"

"Pussy?" I said. "Is there a way we can get up there?" I indicated the high-wire act above our heads.

"If we put all my plush toys in a big pile in the corner we might reach there," said Pussy. "But even if we could, we'd still have to remove the grate."

"I know. But we have to give it a try. It might be our only shot before they come back."

So for the next couple of minutes we created a big pile out of Pussy's plush animals. To our delight there were a lot of them. Like, a great big lot. Finally the pile reached about three quarters to the ceiling, and we took a break to think up the next part of our grand plan.

"I think Dooley should go," said Pussy. "He's the lightest and might reach the highest."

"Agreed," I said.

"You think?" said Dooley. "I think Pussy should try. She's very light on her paws, and will simply whizz through the air like a trapeze artist."

"Why, thank you, Dooley," Pussy said, pleasantly surprised.

"No, I mean it. You could be a ballet dancer for all your grace and beauty."

"Well, I could give it a shot, of course," she said, "but it's really you who should get out of here. I'm not to the one they're going to try and murder."

"Touché," said Dooley, grinning awkwardly for some reason.

"Oh, for crying out loud," I said and gave my friend a nudge in the direction of the pile of plush. "Jump high and aim for that grate over there."

"Aye, aye, captain," said Dooley, licking his lips nervously. He retreated all the way to the opposite corner of the room, then took a long approach and at high speed raced to the pile, hopped up in a few jumps to the top, then took a flying leap in the direction of the grate, and… managed to hang on by his nails!

Unfortunately, two things happened simultaneously: the grate didn't budge, sturdily fastened as it apparently was, and the pile of plush animals, as a consequence of Dooley's ministrations, collapsed and tumbled down.

"Help!" Dooley now bleated, dangling from the ceiling by his nails. "Help me, Max!"

"Oh, hang on, Dooley!" Pussy shouted. "Max will figure something out!"

They both looked at me for aid and comfort, but frankly I drew a complete blank. I mean, I'm not Bruce Willis traipsing all over Nakatomi Plaza!

The only thing I could think of was: "Just let go, Dooley. I'll break your fall."

Just then, two more things happened: the grate finally decided to give up the struggle and dropped out. Dooley, in a supreme demonstration of nimbleness, managed to grab onto the vent opening. And then the door to the room opened and Chris walked in.

The grate fell on top of the man's head, and he went down like a sack of potatoes. And Dooley, up above, quickly disappeared into the vent the moment he heard the door opening and immediately scrabbled out of sight.

"Go, Max!" Pussy shouted. "Now's your chance. Go, go, go!"

And like a speed racer who's been given the all-clear, I bolted for the door. And just when I reached there an obstacle appeared in my path: it was Tank. But since I was going fast and speeding up as I went, I couldn't stop even if I wanted to. Cats don't have inbuilt brakes, so I bumped into Tank at full speed, and since I am easily twice his size it was like a bowling ball hitting a pin: Tank was flung to the side and I still kept going, momentum propelling me through the door.

I was free, and nothing could stop me now!

Except for the maze that was Chateau Leonidas.

Before long I was lost in the warren of corridors, but all the while I kept on running at full tilt, for right behind me was a cat in hot pursuit, and I knew it was Tank, pissed that he'd been bowled over by a mere mongrel like myself.

CHAPTER 22

*O*delia and Chase had been driving along, en route back to town, when suddenly they passed a familiar-looking red car, speeding in the opposite direction, a little old white-haired lady behind the wheel, her face practically plastered against the windshield, a look of determination on her face.

They turned to one another and said in chorus, "Gran."

Odelia performed her second U-turn of the day and moments later was following Gran who, for some reason, was on her way to the Flake house.

The old lady was making good time, though, and no matter how deeply Odelia punched in the accelerator, she wasn't making any headway.

"Where did she go?" cried Chase.

"Gran is in a different category than the rest of the traffic participants," said Odelia through gritted teeth. "She thinks the traffic code is just a suggestion."

"Well, speed up before she wraps her car around a tree."

"Oh, she'll never go and do a silly thing like that," said

Odelia. "She's got the luck of the drunk, even though she doesn't drink."

Finally they were back where they started: at Casa Flake, and to Odelia's elation Gran's car was idling in front of the gate. In spite of her words she'd worried that Chase's predictions might have come true and that she'd find Gran's car wrapped around some indignant tree.

They parked right behind Gran and got out. The old lady was already yelling into the intercom. "Open this gate right now, you shit-for-brains, or I'll come down there and personally rearrange your face!" she was shouting. "Oh, and my cop grandson just arrived and he's going to arrest you and kick your sorry ass into his deepest, darkest dungeon and throw away the key!" she added when she caught sight of Odelia and Chase bearing down on her.

"Don't bother," said Odelia. "They won't let you in."

"They have to, or by golly I'll smite this gate and bring it down!" she said, shaking an irate fist.

And then, suddenly, as if her threats had worked, the gate swung open!

"Glad to see you're back, Kingsley!" a cheerful voice sounded from the intercom. "Forget something, did you?"

"Thanks, buddy!" Chase shouted back.

Apparently whoever had been manning the booth before had now been replaced by Chase's friend, the head of security at the place.

Gran directed her car along the long and winding drive, followed by Odelia and Chase.

"Why are we back here?" asked Chase.

"Um, I have no idea," Odelia confessed. She probably should have asked her grandmother that exact question. Only the moment the gate had swung open Gran had jumped into her car and hared off at the speed of light.

Now she screeched to a halt in front of the house and hopped out, followed by none other than Harriet and Brutus!

"What's the big plan here, Gran?" asked Odelia, also getting out.

"The big plan is to look for Max," said Gran, "and to find out what really happened to this fashion bozo."

"We already looked for Max," said Odelia. "He's not here. And as far as the big fashion bozo is concerned, the guy who killed him is in jail right now."

"Yeah, you don't really think that poor guy had anything to do with this, do you?"

"Actually, I do," said Chase. "Not only did he kill his partner, but he practically confessed, and that's good enough for me, good enough for your son, and I'm willing to bet it's good enough for a judge and a jury of the guy's peers."

"Well, I don't buy it," said Gran.

"Why am I not surprised?" said Chase, throwing up his hands.

"We'll stay here and look for Max, shall we?" Harriet suggested, but Gran was already marching up to the house.

"Yeah, you do that," said Odelia, and went after her grandmother before she got shot or, worse, punched someone in the face and accused them of murder.

"Odelia, we shouldn't be out here," said Chase. "We're trespassing on private property."

"We were invited, remember?" she said.

"Yeah, but that's only because the guard likes your face."

"Likes your face, you mean."

"Also a possibility," Chase admitted. "Still, we're not supposed to be here, and..."

But whatever he'd been about to say would have to wait, for the front door flew open and the lady of the house appeared, seated in her wheelchair, and accompanied by a sturdily-built female nurse with an expressionless face.

"To what do I owe the pleasure?" Mrs. Flake asked.

"You're hiding something, and I'm here to find out what it is," said Gran, throwing down the gauntlet.

"I'm sure I don't know what you're talking about," said the old lady who, if she was shocked by this accusation, didn't show it.

"Oh, I know you tried to take over your son's company," said Gran. "And each time he managed to get you off his back. But you wouldn't give up, would you? And now you finally achieved what you set out to do. You're in charge now, and you're going to run it straight into the ground!"

"Who are you?" asked the woman.

"My name is Vesta Muffin and I'm a private dick!" said Gran, planting both feet on the ground and her hands on her hips.

"She's not a private detective, Leonora," spoke a voice behind the woman. Chris Cross had arrived on the scene. Oddly enough he was rubbing his head, as if he'd bumped it against something, and of his cat there was no sign.

"I am, too," Gran insisted.

"No, you're not. You're a receptionist at your son-in-law's doctor's office and that's all you are. Even your grand-daughter is not a private detective but a reporter, though sometimes she likes to pretend that she's a PI."

"At any rate I'm a cop," said Chase, displaying his badge, "and if you don't mind, can you please answer Mrs. Muffin's questions?"

Cross closed his mouth with a click of the teeth, then said, "You don't have to do this, Leonora. You don't have to say a word to these people."

"It's all right, Chris. I have nothing to hide from this old woman."

"Look who's talking, Mother Time," said Gran.

"The only reason I tried to take over my son's business

was because he managed it in a shoddy way and I wanted to save it from his incompetence."

"Odd," said Gran. "It's been highly profitable for the past thirty years."

"And how would you know? My son did a very good job at hiding the real numbers from his board of directors and his shareholders. I know the real picture and it wasn't pretty. I was doing him a favor by taking over. You see, my son was an artist, a genius, but he had no head for business. And that's where I came in. I ran several companies in my time, and all very successful ones. Together, we would have taken over the world of haute couture."

"Isn't it true that you simply wanted to turn back the clock and make Leonidas Flake all about haute couture again, with no prêt-à-porter collections and no collaborations with the Gap or even Walmart or Costco?" asked Gran.

"Of course I wanted us out of Gap and Costco! Leo was diminishing the value of the brand by selling out. He had to be stopped before the name Leonidas Flake was mud, like so many other formerly great brands."

"I think what happened was that your son was the genius designer, just like you say, and that he indeed didn't have the head for business that you have, but he had a partner who had a feel for the market and who gave Leo the love and affection he needed to soar. And the two of them created magic. "

"Gabriel was the one who got the idea to sell out, if that's what you mean," said Leonora. "He's the one who heralded in the downturn of the once-iconic Leonidas Flake name. It was obvious to me and my advisers that he had to go."

"You got some bad advice, Leonora," said Gran. "Your son's business was flourishing, and Gabe was integral to that success. Instead of saving the company you killed the goose that laid the golden eggs. Just you wait and see."

The corners of the woman's lips turned down. "Are you accusing me of murder, Mrs. Muffin?"

"I'm accusing you of bad judgment. And of being a bad mother."

Leonora's eyes narrowed. "I want you off the premises. All of you." She turned to Chase. "Unless you have a warrant, Detective Kingsley, I want you gone, and please take this raving lunatic with you."

"I'll show you a raving lunatic," said Gran, and actually leaped at the woman! Just before she could land a punch, though, Chase intercepted her.

"Let's go, Vesta," said Chase, leading Gran away with a firm hand.

"She's responsible for her son's death!" said Gran. "I know she is!"

"I wasn't even here when it happened!" the woman shouted. "Ask anyone!"

"She's right," said Chase. "She was at the Hampton Cove Star when her son died. Now let's get out of here before you land us in a big ol' heap of doo-doo."

"What is she going to do?" scoffed Gran. "Call the cops?"

"She might, and I'd probably lose my badge. Now unless you have solid evidence linking her to the death of her son, I suggest we retreat and regroup."

Gran uttered a low growl, but still complied. She shook herself free of Chase's grasp and set foot for the car. "This isn't over, Flake!" she shouted, shaking her fist in the direction of the old woman. "Mark my words!"

"Oh, go away, you crazy old bat," said Leonora, and slammed the door.

Gran got into the car and drove off, kicking up a spray of dust and gravel as she did, and as Odelia and Chase followed her at a more leisurely pace, suddenly Odelia remembered Harriet and Brutus.

"Dang it," she said.

"What's wrong?" asked Chase, who was driving this time.

"Harriet and Brutus. We left them at the house."

"They'll find their way home," said Chase.

And so they would, Odelia thought. And hopefully they'd find Max and Dooley and manage to snap them out of their 'strike.'

CHAPTER 23

I was racing along, trying to find my way out of the maze that Leonidas had built, still persecuted by the sound of a cat in hot pursuit—I could hear his nails scrabbling as he raced along behind me—when suddenly I reached a dead end and almost slammed into a wall. And then the wall slammed into me, or at least that's what it felt like when a solid object and I collided.

The solid object soon turned out not to be all that solid. It was a cat, and before I knew what was happening, I was putting up a fight with the furry fiend, knowing that it was Tank who'd taken a shortcut and who'd managed to intercept my progress. I knew I had to watch out for his claw going for my jugular, and it was only when Tank uttered a loud cry of distress that something registered in my brain and gave me pause.

That cry hadn't sounded like Tank at all.

It had sounded more like Dooley's bleats.

So I halted the proceedings and lo and behold: I was actually fighting my best friend and not, as I had supposed, my mortal enemy!

"Dooley!" I cried.

"Max!" he yelped. "I thought you were Tank!"

"I thought *you* were Tank!"

We fell into each other's arms and before long were laughing at the strange coincidence of both of us thinking we were engaged in the fight of a lifetime against a formidable foe.

"I dropped down from up there," he said, indicating the open vent that gaped overhead and then the grate that had buckled under his weight.

"I thought Tank was chasing me. So that was you?"

"And I thought Tank was chasing me!"

How funny it was, if only our situation hadn't been so dire.

"We still need to get out of here," I said. "Tank probably *is* chasing us."

"Which way is the exit?" asked Dooley, glancing back nervously for a sign of the murderous Siamese.

We both searched around, and suddenly a growling sound came rumbling out of the darkness. There was no doubt this time that it was Tank, and he did not sound happy.

He suddenly stepped into the light, and his eyes glowed red and menacing, his teeth sharp and deadly. His tail was distended and his back was arched and he looked ready to move in for the kill!

"Frankly I've just about had it with this guy," said Dooley, much to my surprise. And before I could stop him, he was charging in the direction of the fearful cat, screaming at the top of his lungs!

"Dooley, no!" I yelled, and then I was racing after my buddy, ready for any fate.

Tank, instead of putting up a fight, saw the two of us

storming towards him, gulped a little, then let out a high squeal, and turned around and ran!

"Huh," I said as we watched him streak off in the direction he came from.

"I guess he's not as tough as he looks," said Dooley, who seemed disappointed that he hadn't been able to engage the horrible cat.

"That was very brave of you, Dooley," I said as I placed my paw on his shoulder. "Probably the bravest thing I've ever seen in my life."

"Sometimes you just have to stand up for yourself, you know."

"You're absolutely right."

We both turned, intent on locating that elusive exit, when suddenly we found ourselves face to face with the biggest, meanest-looking rat I'd ever seen! It was baring its fangs, saliva dripping from the pointy snappers, and it looked about to move in for the kill!

Without a moment's hesitation, Dooley and I turned around and fled the scene—running as fast as our legs could carry us! Before long, we'd reached the staircase, scrambled down at top speed, and kept on running, through the living room, streaked through a crack in the sliding door and out into the open. And as we ran, I thought for a moment I heard Gran's voice. It must have been my imagination, though, for I knew she couldn't possibly be there.

And as Dooley and I stood panting, he said, "So that's why Tank turned and ran! He wasn't afraid of us but of the big, nasty rat!"

"He must have dropped down from that vent—same as you," I said, trying to catch my breath. I'm one of those cats that's built for comfort, not speed, you see, and cardiovascular activity always has a deleterious effect on me.

"Did you hear Gran?" he asked.

"I did."

"We must be hallucinating."

"It's because we were imprisoned. Prisoners often start hearing things."

"Let's go home," said Dooley. "Odelia might not be the ideal human we thought she was, but she's a damn sight better than the people that run this house—or the big, scary rats that infest the ventilation system!"

"I can't believe you were cooped up in there—with that rat!"

"I know!" he said, his eyes wide as saucers.

We both glanced up to the second-floor window of the room we'd just escaped from, and saw to our elation that Pussy was sitting there, looking down at us. And she was smiling!

She held up her paw in greeting, and Dooley shouted, "We're coming back for you, Pussy! We won't leave you there to die!"

Pussy gave us a cheery wave, and then we were off at a trot. Unfortunately we must have taken a wrong turn somewhere, still not fully ourselves after our harrowing ordeal, and before long we found ourselves not on the road to Hampton Cove where home and safety lay, but back in the petting zoo.

"We're back where we started, Max," said Dooley, who'd come to the same conclusion.

"It sure looks that way. Oh, well. I guess all roads lead to Rome," I said.

"They do? And how does that work, exactly?"

"It's just an expression. I don't think all roads literally lead to Rome."

"They'd have to cross an entire ocean, which I think is a little tricky."

And on this note of wisdom, we entered the petting zoo. Any place was better than the Flake house, which had turned out to be a house of horrors.

CHAPTER 24

*L*auren Klepfisch and Zak Kowalski had been staking out the Flake house long enough to know that the place was practically a beehive, with people coming and going at all hours. First a bunch of black SUVs had passed through the gates, probably transporting a US government contingent, or maybe SEAL Team Six, then Odelia Poole had arrived with her cop sidekick, had come and gone, only to return a little while later with her grandmother, before passing out again.

"Something is definitely going on in there," said Lauren, with her reporter's nose for a scoop.

"No shit, Sherlock," said her cameraman. They'd been out there for too long, and Zak was getting a little antsy. He was also hungry for some real food, and not the pizzas they'd had delivered about an hour before.

"I say we move in for a closer look," Lauren suggested. She tapped her nose. "I have a nose for these things, Zak."

"Yeah, like you had a nose for barging into the police station this afternoon and getting kicked out?"

"I may have reacted a little hastily that time."

But she was so sure that they would find a great little scoop there that she'd decided to go for broke and barge into the place. It hadn't worked out so well, and their exclusive interview with Gabriel Crier or Chief Alec or both had been a bust. And now they were forbidden from ever setting foot inside the police station ever again. And after Chief Alec had called Lauren and Zak's boss at WLBC-9, he'd chewed her out and told her in no uncertain terms he was unhappy with her behavior. And if she ever pulled a stunt like that again, she was off the story and off the air. And when she told him she had another scoop, and that Odelia Poole could talk to cats and she could prove it, he'd called her a long list of opprobrious names and slammed down the phone.

Looked like the world wasn't ready to learn Miss Poole's secret yet...

"Let's get the inside scoop," she said. "Something is going on in there and we need to know what it is."

Zak groaned, but he wasn't saying no. A scoop would put food on the table, and maybe even propel him to the next level: a fixed contract. Anything was better than the piece-meal stuff he did now—being paid as a freelancer.

"Let's go for it, Zak," she said. "And if it doesn't work out, I'll tell them it was my fault. I'll take full responsibility."

"Like you will take all the credit if we hit the jackpot, huh? No way, Lauren. We share the credit this time. And no buts."

"Sure. Fine," she said, glad he was willing to follow her into the lion's den. She eyed the fence with a keen eye. "So how high do you think that thing is?"

*L*eonora Flake was staring out across the grounds that backed the estate. It was dark out, so there wasn't a lot to see. She didn't mind. She needed to put all of her ducks in a row. The words of that horrible old woman kept ringing in her ears: you're going to destroy this company with your stupid ideas.

Could she be onto something? Was the reason Leonidas Flake had been as successful as it was, the wedding of two minds: her son and his boyfriend's?

She'd always thought the company was going down the drain, and had tried to save it from Leo's incompetence many times, even if it turned him against her. She'd always justified her actions by arguing she was doing Leo a favor. And now this woman had offered her a completely different view.

She decided to take a little ride through the grounds. It always gave her a fresh perspective to go for an evening stroll, even if stroll wasn't exactly the word that applied to the wheelchair-bound sojourn she liked to undertake.

She lived in her own villa, not far from her son's estate, and also had an apartment in Paris, from where she'd launched her campaign to convince the board that she was the better choice to run the company. It hadn't worked that time, but now it finally had, even if the price was high: the death of her son. It was something that weighed heavily on her mind. She knew she'd miss him, that stubborn mulish man. But she also knew it was all for the best.

At least that's what she'd always thought. She wasn't so sure now.

The numbers didn't lie: Leonidas Flake was in a bad way. But was it in a bad way because of her son's mismanagement, or because of her actions?

She took off along the little dirt path that wound its way through the rolling parkland that stretched out for half a mile in every direction. She soon arrived at what she considered emblematic of her son's silliness: the petting zoo. And as she pushed the wheelchair along the path, she found herself listening to the sounds of the animals. They were soothing sounds, and she had to admit that perhaps there was something to be said for the zoo.

Leo had always told her it calmed his frayed nerves after a long day when surrounded by his little flock, and maybe he had a point. She heard the soft snorts of a horse, the quiet braying of a donkey, and the rustling of straw as the hog dug its snout into its trough. She even heard the grunting of rabbits.

Nice, she thought, and felt her mood improving with leaps and bounds. She'd wanted to get rid of the zoo the moment she took over the house and the company, but now she reflected that maybe she would keep it instead. She'd fired the zookeeper that afternoon, along with the rest of Leo's staff, and had called a local farmer to pick up the animals the next day. Now she might hire a new zookeeper, or rehire the old zookeeper and tell him that she'd made a mistake, and did he want to stay on at half his salary? If he refused, she'd tell him that the animals were all going to the slaughterhouse. He'd quickly agree, as apt as these half-witted animal lovers all were.

Take that stupid cat Pussy, for instance. She couldn't imagine how anyone could love a cat the way Leo and Gabe had. And a pretty hideous cat the creature was at that. With those horrible claws and that terrible cat smell. At least for now, though, she needed to keep the foul beast around. To parade in front of the world's media at next week's press conference, and for the board of directors. But as soon as she didn't need the stupid little bag of bones, it was off to the vet for a lethal injection. Or maybe she would put the thing down herself, and have Pussy buried somewhere on the grounds right next to those other two cats, Max and Dooley. Stupid names for stupid beasts. At least if Chris managed to catch them, which he better had, or else there would be hell to pay. Maybe she'd better ask Helga. Her trusty nurse never messed up.

And she was so lost in thought that she didn't even notice that she'd taken a wrong turn and had gone off the path. She only perceived something wasn't right when she was riding downhill, unable to stop her progress. The next moment she was crashing into a ditch. When she dropped out of her chair and splashed into the water, she screamed, but to no avail. She'd told Helga she wanted to be alone, and of course Leo's security people didn't care what happened to the new owner, since they were all about to be laid off anyway.

Soon she was sinking, and discovered this was no ditch but a pond. And before long the water closed over her head, and she was drowning!

CHAPTER 25

e'd been wandering around the petting zoo for a while, absolutely lost, I don't mind confessing. The problem with being locked up and then escaping by the skin of your teeth is that you're so pumped up on adrenaline that you don't know which way is up or down. We were so elated to be out of our temporary prison that we'd simply been trucking along, without really looking which way we were going. And we were still pottering about the zoo when suddenly loud voices greeted us. They sounded awfully familiar.

"No, I'm telling you, Max would never be seen dead in a pigsty," a female voice said.

"And I'm telling *you* that Max loves all creatures great and small, so this petting zoo is exactly where we'll find him and Dooley."

"Hey, isn't that Harriet?" asked Dooley.

"And Brutus!"

We made for the voices, and when we emerged from a bush found ourselves gazing at a wondrous scene: Harriet and Brutus, sitting next to a very sizable pig!

The pig was munching on something located in a trough, while Harriet and Brutus were arguing back and forth about the strategy they needed to employ to find me and Dooley.

"You guys!" I cried as we burst onto the peculiar scene. "You found us!"

"Max! Dooley!" yelled Harriet, and streaked forward and actually pushed her wet nose into my neck, overjoyed to see me. Displaying affection has never been Harriet's strong suit and it surprised me to see so much of it now.

"Hey, Dooley, old buddy," said Brutus with a grin.

"How did you find us?" asked Dooley.

"Well, you found us," said Brutus, making a good point, "so you tell me."

"Can you guys take this meeting elsewhere?" suddenly spoke the pig in a deep rumbling voice. "You're interrupting a perfectly good meal."

"Oh, I'm so sorry, Mr. Pig," said Dooley. "I apologize for the intrusion."

"Yeah, it's okay," said the pig. "Just don't do it again, will you?"

"Of course," I said.

We moved away from the pigpen and soon found ourselves wandering near a small duck pond. "So what happened?" asked Harriet.

"Oh, we've been hanging out all day in a chicken coop," said Dooley.

"See?!" said Brutus, giving Harriet a light shove. "What did I tell you?"

"The chicken had fled the scene, you see. Her name was Samson," Dooley continued the narrative. "But then we got tired of eating chicken feed, and so we went in search of something tastier and that's when we met Pussy."

In a few words, Dooley and I told the tale of meeting Pussy, attending the conference from the confines of Leo's secret control room, and being locked up and threatened with death by lethal claw by Leonora Flake, Chris Cross and the very scary Tank. Harriet and Brutus were hanging on our every word.

"So they were going to kill you?" asked Harriet. "Actually kill you dead?"

"Yeah, and bury us in a very deep grave," said Dooley.

"Gruesome," said Brutus, duly impressed by our harrowing adventure.

"These are not very nice people," said Dooley. "And Leo's mother is the worst of the bunch."

"Is she behind the whole thing?" asked Brutus.

"You mean did she kill her son?" I said. "That wouldn't surprise me."

"If she can kill a cat, she can kill a human," said Dooley with iron logic.

"She's mean," I agreed. "Capable of just about anything."

Just then, we heard screams and shouts coming from the other side of the pond, and to my surprise it was the same woman we'd been verbally filleting, and who seemed to have landed herself in hot water herself now. Though I should probably say cold water, for as a rule duck ponds are not hot tubs.

"It's Mrs. Flake," I said as we hurried over to where the screams seemed to be coming from. And just as we reached the spot, the woman was going under for the third time, and the only thing that remained were bubbles reaching the surface. Then all was quiet as the watery grave closed above her head...

"We have to save her!" said Harriet.

"Yeah, but how?" I said. Cats, to their detriment, are not equipped with the type of accessories that allow for a water-logged existence: webbed toes and gills and such. Even if we braved all and jumped into the water, what good would it do? We'd probably perish ourselves, and end up at the bottom.

Then Dooley suddenly started yelling his head off. "Heeeeelp!" he screamed. "Heeeeeeelp us!"

I felt bad for the kid. Obviously the day's many brushes with danger and peril had gotten to him, and now he'd lost what little sanity he had left.

Soon, though, a cow waddled up to take a closer look.

"What's going on?" she asked in her customary amiable way.

"Somebody's drowning!" Dooley said. "You have to help her!"

"Ooh, that's a job for Francis," she said, then displaced a wad of grass from one cheek to the other and hollered, "Francis! We've got a jumper!"

Francis the donkey came toddling up, and directed a curious look at the pond. "No can do," he said after a moment's deliberation. "Too deep for me, I'm afraid. But maybe Streaker can handle it. Streaker! Come here a minute, will ya?"

Streaker the horse came cantering up. "Yes? Yes?" she said, eager for any fate. It was obvious that here was a horse dying to get some serious action.

"Jumper," said Francis, indicating the pond with his hoof.

"Ooh, wee!" said Streaker happily, and jumped headfirst into the pond!

Moments later she returned grabbing the old lady between her large teeth, then proceeded to drag her onto the shore!

"Way to go, Streaker," said Brutus with admiration.

"Now we need to do CPR," said Dooley, happy that his plan was working but still not fully satisfied with the outcome.

"CPR?" asked Streaker eagerly. "What is CPR? Can I do it? Please?"

"Thump her chest and then put your lips on hers," said Brutus, "and blow."

"Thump, lips and blow," said Streaker excitedly. "I can do it."

"Let me handle this, fellas," said the pig, who'd joined the festivities. "I have the build for this kind of thing." And so she heaved herself down on the woman's chest for a moment, then put her lips to Leonora's and blew hard.

"Nothing doing," she said after a moment. "Looks dead to me."

"Well, don't you just stand there!" Francis told two sheep who'd come shambling up. "You perform heart massage while Empress does her thing."

The pig, whose name appeared to be Empress, gave a curt nod of agreement, and soon the sheep showed a side of themselves I'd rarely seen in the Discovery Channel's nature movies: they gently put their front hooves on the woman's chest and started performing heart massage while Empress kept blowing into the woman's mouth.

"Let me do it!" said Streaker. "I can do it! Let me do it!"

"Shush," said Francis, who seemed to be the donkey in charge. "Empress is a natural. She'll pull this off—just you wait and see."

And then, suddenly, a miracle! The corpse came to life again with a start: first she spewed out a stream of mucky pond scum, and then she actually started sputtering and coughing. The ducks, who'd been awakened by all this activity, waddled up onto the shore, took one look at the drowning victim, then waddled off again. They obviously had no sympathy for landlubbers.

"Yesss!" said Francis. "We did it, you guys. She's saved!"

"How are you doing, ma'am?" inquired Empress politely.

"Anything else I can help you with? I have some nice slop in my trough you're welcome to."

Mrs. Flake stared at the pig with a horrified expression on her face. Unfortunately the pig mistook the look she gave her for a cry for help, and so put her lips to Mrs. Flake's again, and blew some more hot air into her lungs.

"Blech!" the woman uttered curtly, and frantically wiped her lips. And then she threw up some more pond scum, showing us how alive she really was.

"A success story, you guys," said the cow happily.

"A miracle," said one of the sheep, and bleated its delight.

"Teamwork!" said Francis the donkey.

"Is there anyone else in the water?" asked Streaker. "A man? A girl? A boy? I can get them for you! I can do it—I swear! I can do it!"

"You saved me?" Mrs. Flake asked, glancing around at the nativity scene.

"Yup, we sure did," said a goat, who'd only now joined the gang.

Two rabbits came hopping up. "What's going on? Did we miss the party?"

"If you like I'll jump in and save you all over again!" Streaker cried excitedly.

"It's all right, Streaker," said Francis. "You did good."

"I know I did—and I can do it again in a flash!"

Mrs. Flake now stared at the four of us, seated in a neat row: Dooley, yours truly, Harriet and Brutus.

"You saved me?" she asked again. "After everything I did to you?"

"Oh, well," I said. "We don't like to hold a grudge."

"Yeah, we're all human, after all," said Dooley.

"Forgive and forget and all that," added Brutus.

And then, to my surprise, Leo's mother actually burst into tears!

"She's probably just realized she lost her wheelchair," said Dooley.

"A wheelchair?" asked Streaker. "Where is it? Where! Tell me!"

"Still in the pond," I said. "Must have sunk to the bottom by now."

"Hop in, Streak. Fetch," said Francis with an indulgent smile.

"I'm on it!" Streaker cried, and jumped into the pond. Moments later she came out with the wheelchair clasped between her teeth. "Here you go, ma'am!" she said as she deposited the contraption next to the old lady.

The wheelchair was covered in muck and looked a little worse for wear.

"Some love from the high-pressure hose and it's as good as new," said Francis, who'd noticed the same.

"Oh, I'm such a horrible person," said Mrs. Flake, shaking her head mournfully. "I killed my own son!"

"You did?" I said, surprised at this impromptu confession.

"He was doing such a lousy job with the company and I had a feeling he was dragging us all down and if I didn't get rid of him I'd go down with the ship. I own thirty percent of the company, and my shares were going to be worthless if Leo kept this up—or at least that's what my advisors told me."

"Killing your own son, huh? That wasn't very nice of you," grunted Francis.

"Can she understand what we're saying?" asked Harriet.

"I don't think so," I said. "But I guess she feels like confessing."

"She almost died," said Francis. "It's a pivotal moment for her."

"I didn't kill him myself, of course," Leonora said now. "I told my nurse to do it for me. I could never have held the knife that took my son's life. Besides, I was persona non grata at the chateau. But Helga wasn't. She simply swapped shifts with one of Leo's nurses and gave Gabe a sedative. She then planted the knife in his hands and made sure he was at the scene just as the maid walked in. The whole thing was arranged like clockwork. Helga is German, you see," she said, as if this explained everything. "She's been with me for so long she's like a daughter to me. She'd do everything for me. So when I told her I needed to get rid of my boy, she immediately understood and arranged the whole thing with impeccable precision and efficiency."

"So she was the one who plunged the knife into your son's chest?" I asked.

"It was a little hard to juggle all the different elements, of course," Mrs. Flake went on. "But I knew for a fact that my son is a stickler for punctuality, and liked his maid to wake him up every morning at seven o'clock on the dot. So all Helga had to do was make sure that Gabe was standing there, knife in hand, at seven o'clock sharp, and the deal was done. It wasn't hard. The hard part, she later told me, was to drive that knife into his heart. She hit bone, you see, and since she only had a very short window of time, she got a little nervous at some point. Especially since my son woke up at that moment and started to scream. She managed in the end, though. It all worked out fine."

"Define fine," mumbled Brutus.

"We should probably call the police," said Dooley.

"Take out your phone, Dooley," said Harriet. "I forgot mine at the house."

Dooley actually reached around, before realizing Harriet was playing a little joke on him. "Oh, ha ha," he said. "You don't have a phone, do you?"

"No, I don't. And neither do you."

"Oh, no," said Leonora, burying her face in her hands. "What have I done?"

All the animals were quiet as they listened to the woman unburdening her soul. It wasn't a pleasant tale to hear, and I'm sorry to say I didn't feel a lot of compassion for Mrs. Flake. The only thing I was sorry about was that we didn't have anyone to witness her confession, for as you may or may not know, the word of a cat, or a cow, a pig, a horse, a donkey or even a sheep, goat or rabbit, for that matter, doesn't carry a lot of weight in a court of law.

And for a moment I feared that this whole exercise was in vain, when suddenly two people popped up from a nearby bush, one of them holding a camera, the other a microphone, and abruptly descended on the scene.

"Are you sorry now, Mrs. Flake, that you gave the order to murder your son?" asked the woman, whose eyes were glittering with excitement.

Leo's mom stared at the woman, then at the camera, then broke down into a flood of tears again.

Yep. The jig was up.

CHAPTER 26

A week had passed since the stirring events at Chateau Leonidas and we'd all had a little time to reflect on the incidents that had transpired at the house of that celebrated and now mourned couturier. We were in Marge and Tex's backyard, where Tex was working away at the grill, preparing us one of his excellent meals. I must say that in all the years I've been with the Pooles, I'd never seen him more excited. Marge had recently bought him a new grill, some state-of-the-art contraption, ostensibly for his birthday, but we all knew her secret hope was that it would magically turn him into a better grill master.

Unfortunately there were still a few kinks to work out, and the upshot was that the patties Tex threw on the grill, or the steaks and ribs, for that matter, were instantly turned to ash and not the culinary feast Marge had anticipated when she forked over the money for the Webber Master-Touch 2010102b.

Good thing Uncle Alec had the presence of mind to call his buddy Bud Bouchard over in the neighboring town of Happy Bays, and have that stalwart butcher whip up a nice spread. If Tex was embarrassed by this fiasco, he didn't show it. And it was my impression he had every intention to keep grilling away at his new cool toy until there was no more meat left in the world.

Alec was seated at the table, along with Marge, Tex, Odelia, Chase and Gran, while the cat population was relegated to the kids' table, or in our case, the porch, where we occupied the swing. One extra plate had been set out—or rather a bowl—for Pussy, who was our guest of honor. And at the table for the grownups a human guest was seated: it was none other than Gabriel Crier, who'd been invited by Uncle Alec and Chase, to make up for the gross miscarriage of justice which had almost taken place under their auspices.

"Amazing flavor," said Pussy as she dug her teeth into a nugget of meat.

"Tastes a damn sight better than Tex's ash flavor," Brutus chimed in.

"It's the gesture that counts," said Dooley.

"Yeah," I agreed. "Tex has his heart in the right place, even though he's not exactly the world's best grill master."

Odelia came over to check on us, and when she saw we were all tucking in with relish, crouched down next to me, and whispered, "Can you ever forgive me, buddy?"

"Oh, but I forgave you a long time ago, Odelia," I said, and I meant it. Moments after those reporters had come springing from the bushes, the sound of a police siren had told us they hadn't merely filmed Leonora's confession but had also done the right thing by calling in the cavalry.

Soon cops were crawling all over the petting zoo, accompanied by Odelia and Chase and Gran, who'd scooped us up into their arms and had hugged us and kissed us and held us as if they'd missed us for days and days. And when Dooley and I had told them our adventures, Odelia had actually cried. Her distress was short-lived, though, when Pussy joined us, and had related the tale of our heroic escape attempt and how Dooley had been the hero of the hour. And when I related how Dooley had actually saved Mrs. Flake's life by calling for help, Odelia had hugged him so close his ribs had actually creaked.

"I'm sorry I neglected you guys," she said now, for the hundredth time. "It was never my intention. It's just that between work and Chase and things I kinda got distracted."

"You have to keep your eye on the ball," said Pussy. "That's what Leo taught me. Never take your eye off the ball or the whole thing might fall apart."

"Words to live by," Dooley said, putting a piece of sausage into his mouth.

"He also told me never to eat sausage because you never know what they put into those things and the skin is made from the bowels of a dead pig."

Dooley spat out the piece of sausage.

Pussy laughed. "Just kidding!" she said, then grew serious. "Or am I?"

"Fun times," said Brutus with a grin.

"I'm going to make up for my sins by taking you all out next weekend," said Odelia now.

"Out? Where?" I asked.

"To Banner's Farm," she said with a smile.

We all yipped. Gabe had put Chateau Leonidas up for sale. He didn't want to keep on living there since it reminded him too much of the happy times with his partner. The animals who'd inhabited the small zoo had been transferred to Banner's Farm, where visitors could interact with them, and where kids could attend workshops and even help feed the animals.

"Am I also invited?" asked Pussy timidly.

"Of course," said Odelia. "It wouldn't be the same without you, Pussy."

Gabe was now officially Pussy's guardian, and together they actually ran the company, with a little help from Odelia, who was able via Skype to relay Pussy's input to Gabe.

Chris had been relegated to jail, with Tank now spending his days in the care of Chris's mom, who was a strict disciplinarian, and wasn't taking any nonsense from the nasty little brute. Leonora was also in jail awaiting trial. Her confession had been headline news, and even though she kept screaming fake news, and claiming the whole thing had been created with Photoshop, there wasn't a person who believed her. Especially since Helga had decided to come clean and confess what she'd done. It ended a particularly sordid history in the annals of Hampton Cove, one we were all glad to leave behind us.

Odelia straightened and joined the humans at their table.

"I still think we should set up a detective agency," Gran was saying.

"You mean you and me?" said Odelia.

"Of course you and me, and Max, Dooley, Harriet and Brutus. Whatever that guy Chris Cross was doing we can do, too. Only much, much better."

"It's an idea," said Chase carefully.

"I like it," said Tex. "The Pet Detective Agency. PDA."

They all laughed at that, except Tex, who didn't get the joke.

"It's going to attract a lot of attention," said Marge. "And potentially a lot of negative publicity."

"Yeah, I don't think it's a good idea, Gran," said Odelia. "We'll get a ton of crackpots who are drawn in by the publicity. I think we should continue the way we have, out of the limelight, and keeping things as discreet as we can."

"I guess so," said Gran grudgingly.

"You don't want to subject your cats to that kind of scrutiny," Uncle Alec said. "It will bring in kidnappers and all kinds of weirdos and nutcases who might try to grab the cats and hang them on their walls as trophies."

I shivered at the word picture Uncle Alec had painted. Not a pretty one.

"What are trophies, Max?" asked Dooley.

"The heads of animals that hunters like to collect so they can show off to their friends how good they are at murdering animals."

Now Dooley shivered, too. "How terrible!"

How terrible, indeed.

"You know, I can't thank you guys enough," said Gabe. "If not for you, I'd still be in prison and the company would have probably been run into the ground by Leonora."

"Yeah, she was misguided when she thought she would do a better job than you and Leo," said Odelia.

"Sadly she was misinformed," said Gabe. "Apparently some of the shareholders had been feeding her the wrong kind of information for years, and she truly believed that Leo and I were destroying the company, and the only way to save it was to get rid of Leo and myself."

"Sad story," said Marge as she ladled a large helping of potato salad onto the former hair stylist's plate.

"Yeah, if only I'd known what she was up to," said Gabe. "I might have been able to stop her."

"You can't think that way, Gabe," said Marge.

"Marge is right," said Tex. "Thinking like that will drive you nuts."

Alec clapped the other man on the back, almost making him choke on a piece of potato salad. "I knew you didn't do it, buddy. Call it a cop's hunch."

"You seemed pretty convinced, Alec," said Chase.

"Oh, in my heart of hearts I knew all along Gabe wasn't our guy."

"Good to know!" said Gabe laconically, eliciting a grin from Chase and a frown from Alec.

"So this is the second time our lack of swimming skills has hampered us," I said.

"Wasn't Odelia going to teach us how to swim?" asked Brutus.

"She was, but I'm not exactly looking forward to it," said Harriet. "Imagine this fur, wet. It's going to be a tragedy."

"It's not a joke," said Pussy when Dooley laughed. "If I get wet my fur soaks up water like a sponge and I turn into a balloon. Drags me right down."

"Only short-haired cats should swim," said Brutus. "Like you and me, Dooley."

"I'm not sure," said Dooley, not all that keen on becoming a swimmer.

"By the way," I said, "when are we going to be able to congratulate you two?"

Harriet frowned. "What are you talking about?"

"The kittens," said Dooley, catching my drift. "You were going to adopt."

Harriet and Brutus shared a quick look, then Harriet shook her head. "We've thought about it and we've decided to wait."

"Wait?" asked Dooley. "Wait for what?"

"For later, all right? And now can you please shut up about kittens already?!"

Dooley shut up. I could have told him that Harriet was the kind of cat who, once she got an idea into her head, could drive everyone crazy harping on about it, but just as soon forgot all about it when a new idea entered her head. I had the impression she'd forgotten about those kittens the moment she'd mentioned them, and didn't enjoy being reminded of her impetuousness.

"I like kittens," said Pussy dreamily.

"Hey, I like kittens!" said Dooley.

"What a coincidence!" Pussy cried.

"I like kibble," said Dooley.

"Me, too!"

The two stared at each other for a moment, then Pussy giggled, and so did Dooley, and if I wasn't mistaken, he actually blushed beneath his fur.

Oh, dear. This could only mean one thing. Dooley was in love.

"Let's give these two lovebirds some space, Max," said Brutus with all the delicacy and diplomacy of an elephant stomping on someone's toes.

But he was probably right. Still, it was with some reluctance that I followed Harriet and Brutus and left Dooley and Pussy to explore what else they had in common, aside from their self-professed love of kittens and kibble.

And as I walked away I could see the love light shining brightly in Dooley's eyes.

"Let's slip next door, snuggle bunny," said Harriet, on whom young love always had an aphrodisiacal effect.

"Great idea, angel face," grunted Brutus.

And before I knew what was happening, I suddenly found myself all by myself. And as I wandered into the fallow piece of land lining Odelia's backyard, I was feeling slightly dejected. If my best friend was going to hook up with the richest cat in the world, what was going to happen to me? And as I aimlessly drifted here and there, I suddenly noticed a pair of cat's eyes following my every movement. When I looked over, I saw they belonged to a cat I knew very well indeed.

"Hey, Clarice," I said. "How are things?"

"Things could literally not be better," she said.

Clarice is a feral cat who likes to live wild and free. She roams the fields and forests surrounding Hampton Cove, and is the best dumpster diver I know. She's also something of an acquired taste. And she has a standing invitation, extended by Odelia, to consider our house her home.

"Care for a piece of succulent meat?" I asked.

"Is Tex manning the grill?"

"No. They hired a caterer."

"Then I don't mind if I do," she said, and followed me into the backyard.

She watched as Dooley and Pussy got cozy, and clicked her tongue. "Young love," she said. "It disgusts me."

I laughed. "Most people wouldn't agree with that particular view."

"That's because most people are idiots."

"Well, if not for young love no babies would be born, or kittens."

"And would that be such a bad thing?"

What did I tell you? Acquired taste.

We moved over to Odelia's side and when Odelia saw Clarice she smiled and petted her. Odelia is the only one who is allowed to do that, and Clarice actually purred with delight!

Odelia then handed down a piece of burger and Clarice gobbled it up. "Keep em coming," she snarled, and Odelia did just that.

Clarice then jumped up on Odelia's lap, and the feast continued unabated.

And as I watched on, Clarice being fed and petted by Odelia, Dooley and Pussy gabbing away on the swing, my humans prattling gaily in the backyard, and Brutus and Harriet ducking in and out of the shrubbery, my heart warmed. Who was I kidding? Even if Dooley hooked up with Pussy, which I kinda doubted he would, I wasn't losing a friend but gaining another friend.

"I kinda like this human of yours, Max," Clarice grunted. "If you're tired with her, I just might adopt her for my own."

"No way," I said. "Odelia is mine."

"Hah," said Clarice with a sly grin. "I knew you'd say that."

"Max!" Dooley shouted. "Pussy likes naps, and I like naps, too! How about that!"

"God," said Clarice, shaking her head. "This is torture."

"And I hate getting wet and Dooley hates getting wet, too!" Pussy said.

"And guess what? There's something else we have in common!" Dooley said.

"Yeah, we both like you, Max!" Pussy said.

"We love you, buddy!" said Dooley.

I held up my paw. Somehow I'd suddenly lost my voice.

I swiped at my eyes. Tears, you ask? Nah. Just a speck of dust. In both eyes.

EXCERPT FROM PURRFECT TRAP
(THE MYSTERIES OF MAX 15)

Prologue

Heavy rain lashed the windows of the homes that lined the road. A storm had blown in overnight and the wind had picked up speed. Lightning slashed the sky and the night was black as ink. Elon Pope, as he pushed down on the pedals of his bicycle, cursed his decision to take his bike and not the Lambo. He could have been home by now, warm and dry, heating himself by the family fireplace. But no, he had to play the hero again.

When his sister Marcie had accused him of being a climate denier and a grade-A polluter, he'd pointed out to her that he wasn't merely the proud owner of a Maserati and a Lamborghini but also of a good old-fashioned bike, so when she'd challenged him to hit the pubs on his bike and leave his supercars at home, he'd foolishly taken her on.

And now here he was, riding along this deserted stretch of road in the middle of the night, while Hampton Covians were all safely tucked into their beds, pedaling away like a madman. His nice Moreschi shoes were ruined, his black

Armani jeans spattered and caked with mud and muck, and his favorite Ralph Lauren polo shirt completely soaked.

His hair was plastered to his skull and he had trouble seeing which way he was going from the rain lashing his face and running into his eyes. Oh, damn you, Marcie.

Soon he'd left Hampton Cove behind, and was traveling along one of the smaller roads out of town. No posh residences here, though—only a bunch of old houses and rundown farms. One of those old houses was his family home, and the knowledge that he was close made him push down on those pedals with renewed fervor. One more mile.

And he'd just reached a fork in the road, and taken a left turn, when suddenly lightning flashed once again, only this time hitting much closer. It actually struck a willow tree close by and the sparks made Elon utter an inadvertent yelp of fear.

Yikes. This horrible storm was not only inconvenient but also seriously dangerous! Hadn't he once read about a man being struck by lightning in just such a storm? And what had the advice been? To hide under a tree? Or not to hide under a tree? He couldn't remember. One thing he shouldn't do was stand still in the middle of the street. Or ride an iron bicycle on the open road... He looked around for a moment, wondering whether to go on or to take cover for a moment. Maybe let the worst of the storm blow over.

He wiped the rain from his eyes and glanced over to the old Buschmann house, just beyond the bend. Rumor had it that the place was haunted by the ghost of old Royce Buschmann. Nonsense, of course. Old man Buschmann had simply died and the house had fallen into disrepair, its owner having had no children or siblings to inherit the place.

Lightning struck once more, eerily illuminating the old structure. He shivered, and not just from being soaked through and through. It was almost as if the house had a soul.

As if an evil entity possessed it. Even as a child he'd never been able to pass the house without a shiver, and to this day he preferred to take the other road into town, and avoid this part of the neighborhood.

He didn't look away, though. For some reason he couldn't, his gaze inexorably drawn to that hideous facade, those dormer windows like eyes, that gaping mouth for a door.

He suddenly realized that he'd stopped, and instead of bicycling away from the house as fast as his chilled legs could carry him, he was actually getting off his bike and approaching the house, as if some dark and mysterious force compelled him.

Thunder made the earth quake, and he snapped out of his strange reverie.

He'd simply had one too many to drink, and wasn't thinking straight right now.

And that's when he saw it: a pale face was staring right back at him from inside the house! A horrible face with eyes black as coal. It was old man Buschmann himself!

But before he could drag his eyes away from the hideous sight, something exploded across his skull. A sudden pain bloomed at the back of his head. And he knew no more.

Chapter One

"Well, you can't have it."

"Yes, I can!"

"Over my dead body!"

"That can be arranged!"

I sat watching the spectacle like a spectator at the US Open.

"Who are you rooting for, Max?" asked Dooley, who was sitting next to me and enjoying the same show.

"I'm not sure," I confessed. "Normally I'd root for Tex, as he often seems to be the voice of reason in this crazy family, but I feel that Gran has a point, too."

"I agree," said Dooley, which wasn't a big surprise. After all, Grandma Muffin is his human, and if only out of a sense of self-preservation cats often take the side of the humans that feed them. Hypocritical, I know, but there you go.

"I need one of those new-fangled smartphones and if you won't buy me one I'm moving out!"

"Fine!" said Tex. "Move out if you want. See if I care!"

The two opponents stood at daggers drawn, both with their arms crossed in front of their chests, and their noses practically touching.

"I need that phone!" Gran tried again, clearly not as keen on moving out as her threat had promised.

"No, you don't. You have a perfectly functioning smartphone and that'll have to do!"

We were in Marge and Tex's kitchen, where all good fights between Tex and his mother-in-law usually take place.

"My phone is old—I need a new one."

"It's not old—it's practically brand-new!"

"It's five years old! It's an antique!"

"My phone is five years old, and you don't hear me complaining."

"That's because you're an antique yourself."

"Sticks and stones, ma. Sticks and stones."

"You probably got my phone at a frickin' yard sale!"

In actual fact Tex had bought Gran's phone on eBay, but he wasn't going to let an insignificant little detail like that derail a perfectly good fight.

"It's as good as new, and it'll have to do."

"It's an iPhone five! They're already up to ten or eleven!"

"So? If every time Apple comes out with a new iPhone I have to buy you one, I'd be broke!"

He had a point, and Dooley murmured his agreement, as did I. At the rate these smartphone manufacturers kept putting out new models you could spend a fortune, especially as they kept getting more and more expensive. The latest ones cost well over a thousand bucks. A thousand dollars for a silly little gadget! Nuts. It just goes to show that there's no limit to the avarice of your latter-day capitalist when he hits on a guileless public willing to part with its hard-earned cash. Or, in this case, Tex's hard-earned cash.

"Ma, you don't need a new phone," said Marge, also entering the argument, albeit reluctantly, as nothing good ever came from getting into a fight with her mother.

Grandma Muffin may look like a sweet old granny, with her little white curls and her angelic pink face, but underneath all that loveliness lurks a tough old baby.

"It folds!" Gran now yelled.

Both Tex and Marge stared at her. "It does what now?" asked Tex.

"The new phones! They fold right down the middle. And I want one."

Tex rolled his eyes, and so did Marge. A collective eye roll. Not good.

"You don't need a foldable smartphone, ma," said Marge.

"Yeah, those things are fragile," said Tex. "Plus they cost a fortune."

"I need the bigger screen, so I can watch my shows on my phone."

Gran is an avid consumer of soap operas. I think she watches all of them, if she has the chance. And the ones she can't watch, on account of the fact that she works at Tex's doctor's office as a receptionist, she records on her DVR and watches later in the day.

"You can watch your shows on the TV like a normal person," said Tex.

"I want to watch them live at the office. It's different when you watch them live."

"Someone should tell Gran that none of those shows are live," I said.

Instead, Marge wagged her finger at her mother. "You shouldn't watch shows when you're working, ma."

"Well, I want to, and I will," Gran said stubbornly. "There's never much to do at the office in the afternoon. Besides, Tex's patients bore me, with all their yapping about their irritable bowel syndrome and their hemorrhoids. Who cares about some old idiot's bowels! I don't need that crap in my life. I want my shows and I want to watch them live."

"She's right," said Dooley. "She always misses her favorite shows these days."

"All working people miss their favorite shows," I pointed out. "That's what DVRs are for. Besides, she can watch them online. Most networks put shows online these days."

Frankly the whole argument was starting to get a little tedious, not to mention repetitive, so I decided to leave them to it, and move into the living room, where a couch was waiting that had my name on it. Well, not literally, of course. But it is very comfy.

Dooley felt the same way, for he followed me out, the voices of three adults yelling at each other over a foldable smartphone following us into the living room. We hopped up onto the couch, turned around a couple of times to find ourselves the perfect spot, and finally lay down, neatly folding our tails around our faces, and promptly dozed off.

You're probably wondering why I wasn't over at Odelia's, enjoying my perfectly good nap on my own perfectly good couch. Well, I will tell you why. Odelia and Chase are redecorating, and the house is a total mess right now. Not only that, but there's a weirdly annoying smell of wallpaper glue and paint that pervades the entire house, and it fills me with such a sense of nausea I have trouble finding sleep. So for the time being Dooley and I have both decided to seek refuge at Tex and Marge's. Fights are never pleasant, unless you love their entertainment value, like we do, but the stench of paint fumes is actually a lot worse, and even deleterious for one's general health and well-being.

And I'd just dozed off and had started dreaming about the birds and bees—real birds and bees, mind you—when a loud booming voice practically had me tumbling down from my high perch. I was up and poised in a fight-or-flight position, ready for any contingency, when I saw that the booming voice didn't actually belong to a human presence in the room, but to some loudmouth on the television, which Gran had just switched on and was watching intently, the volume cranked up to maximum capacity.

"Gran! Turn that down!" Tex bellowed from the kitchen.

But Gran decided to play deaf, and sat watching the TV with a mulish expression on her face. Obviously foldable smartphone negotiations hadn't reached a breakthrough.

"Max?" said Dooley.

"Uh-huh?" I said, my heart rate slowly climbing down from its Himalayan heights.

"Isn't that the guy?"

"What guy?" I said, wishing not for the first time that cats were able to put their fingers in their ears, the way humans can.

"The guy on the TV."

I redirected my attention to the television for the first time. Apart from the noise, I hadn't really paid any attention to the particular spectacle that was unfolding there.

The evening news was on, and newscaster Lauren Klepfisch, a lady we'd met in a recent adventure, was announcing that a person had gone missing, and asking the public to keep an eye out for him. I have to admit I didn't recognize the youth in question. He was liberally pimpled and had a big zit on the tip of his nose. Not the picture of beauty.

"I don't think I've had the pleasure..." I began.

"The lottery guy," said Dooley. "The kid who won the lottery."

I stared at the picture of the youth some more. According to the report his name was Elon Pope, and apart from the pimples he was also red-bearded and a little portly. In fact he looked like a younger, chunkier Ed Sheeran. He was grimacing awkwardly into the camera, a hunted expression in his eyes. It was one of those pictures paparazzi like to snap of unsuspecting celebrities. Paparazzi just love to make celebrities look like fools, and they must have had a field day with Elon Pope. His entire expression screamed deer in the headlights, and I wondered if they'd caught him exiting some local den of inequity or other house of disrepute. And then I recognized him. "Hey, isn't that..."

"One of the youngest kids ever to win the lottery," said Gran, who was following the story with rapt attention, her anger at being denied Tim Cook's latest toy a distant memory.

"That's right," I said. "How much did he win again?"

"Three hundred million and change," said Gran with a wistful look on her face. "You can buy a lot of foldable smartphones with three hundred million and change," she added, indicating Tim Cook's toy shop was still very much at the forefront of her mind.

According to the report Elon had vanished without a trace. He'd last been seen exiting the Café Baron, the hipster bar on Downey Street, but never made it home.

"Maybe he decided to disappear," Dooley suggested.

"Could be," Gran agreed.

Dooley might be on to something. The kid hadn't expected to win the big pot and had been struggling in the aftermath of his big win. At twenty-one, he'd immediately walked out of his job at the 7-Eleven where he'd made a career as a shelf stacker, and never looked back. But then stories had started to surface about the fancy house he bought, and the fleet of fancy cars he acquired, and the models he'd been dating, and the wild and crazy parties he'd been throwing, where a bunch of strangers he'd never met before but who'd suddenly become his best friends forever had enjoyed his lavish hospitality.

"He probably decided enough was enough," said Gran. "Or else he ran out of money already, and decided to move to Mexico and start a new life as a shelf stacker over there."

She then resolutely switched the channel to *Jeopardy*, and for the next half hour intently followed the exciting exploits of Alex Trebek as he guided us through another series of tough questions to guess. To Gran's credit, she guessed every last one of them.

But Dooley and I had had enough. Gran's habit of turning the volume up to the max was impeding with our natural predilection for peace and quiet, so we decided to leg it.

We hopped down from the couch and moved upstairs to Gran's room, which was devoid of both noise and humans, curled up at the foot of her bed and were soon fast asleep once more.

Ah, blisssss...

It wasn't long, though, before the world decided to intrude upon our slumber. This time not in the form of Lauren Klepfisch or Alex Trebek, but our fellow cats Harriet and Brutus.

"What are you guys doing in here?" asked Harriet, who looked annoyed by our presence, even though technically she was the one who was intruding.

"We're trying to get some quality Z's," I said pointedly. "What are you doing here?"

"Haven't you heard?" said Brutus. "Odelia has decided to take us all to Vena's again, so we figured we'd hide in the last place she would look."

I gulped, and so did Dooley. Vena Aleman is Hampton Cove's number-one veterinarian, and Odelia always finds some excuse to take us there and have us turned inside out by Vena's gloved hands. More often than not discomfort and pain is involved, not to mention needles and all manner of torture gear. Suffice it to say we don't like Vena, and we don't like this habit of Odelia of dragging us there, even when we're not sick.

"Oh, my God," I said, raising my paws. "Why can't she just leave us alone?!"

"Right?" said Harriet. "All of us are the picture of health, but still she insists on having us checked out over and over and over again. And Vena never finds a thing!"

"Exactly!" I cried, indignation making me sound squeaky. Like a squirrel.

"You have been having trouble chewing lately, though, Max," said Dooley.

"No, I haven't," I said quickly.

"Yeah, you have," said Brutus. "You told me so yourself."

"Yeah, and you keep favoring your left side, because of the pain on the right," said Harriet.

"I'm sure it's nothing," I said, my paws breaking out into a sweat. "It will pass."

I should never have told Dooley, or Harriet, or Brutus! Of course they would go blabbing to Odelia and now she was taking me to Vena's and I was for it! For it!

"You should have that tooth checked out, Max," Dooley said now. "It's not good for you to keep walking around with a bad tooth."

"You guys, I keep telling you, I don't have a bad tooth! It's all good, I'm fine!" They gave me a look of pity that almost hurt as much as my tooth was hurting. "I swear!" I said. "It doesn't hurt. Look!" I chewed down on the comforter. "Do you think I would do this if my tooth hurt? Huh?"

"It's very soft, this comforter," said Harriet skeptically. "Try biting down on this."

She pointed to Gran's wooden footboard. I flinched, then decided to accept the challenge, and bit down on the board, which was about half an inch of laminated chipboard. Immediately I regretted my initiative, as a sharp pain shot through my jaw, then blossomed into my head like a full-blown headache. Ouch! I let go of the board and had to grit my teeth to keep from uttering a yelp. Of course by gritting my teeth I only made matters worse, and when the faces of my friends contorted in a vicarious pain response, I cried, "Okay, so my tooth hurts a little bit! But so what? It will heal, right?"

"Wrong," said Harriet, who was quickly becoming the voice of unreason. "Teeth don't heal by themselves, Max. They should be looked at by a professional."

"Like Vena," said Dooley helpfully.

"So you're going to the vet, buddy," said Brutus. "Whether you like it or not."

"In fact we're all going," said Harriet, patting my back.

"To give you the emotional support you need," Dooley added.

I shook off Harriet's paw. "I'm not going and that's my final word," I said. "In fact if I never set foot in Vena's office ever again it will be too soon!"

Chapter Two

Vena was making a face, which told me things with my tooth weren't as good as I'd imagined.

"This isn't good," she said, as if she'd read my mind. Then made a tsk-tsking sound.

"Oh, poor Maxie," said Odelia. She still had a few splashes of paint on her face, and wallpaper glue in her hair. Also with us at the doctor's office were, as promised, Dooley, Harriet and Brutus. For moral support, though judging from their faces and the rapt attention they now paid to the procedure, they were more there as rubberneckers and disaster tourists. You know. The kind of cats that enjoy train wrecks and car crashes.

"Is it bad?" I finally asked around Vena's gloved fingers as they probed my gums and caused me no small degree of discomfort and pain.

"Oh, how sweet," said Vena, who could only hear my meows.

Odelia, on the other hand, understands what cats are saying, and she translated my thoughts to the medical woman. "Is it bad, Vena?" she asked.

"You better believe it, baby," said the large woman. Vena is cut from the same mold that produced the likes of John Cena and Arnold Schwarzenegger and could probably have been a pro wrestler if she hadn't decided to become a professional pet torturer instead. She was shaking her head in abject dismay. "He must have been in a lot of pain for a long time. Three teeth are beyond salvage. Broken off, protruding roots, infected gum, pus dripping from an abscess. Here. I'll show you," she said, and probed my painful gum with obvious delight. "See? And here. See how swollen his gums are?"

I had half a mind to bite down on her fingers, but decided not to. Not out of the goodness of my own heart, mind you, but because I didn't want to risk hurting my teeth even more. Vena was right. I had been suffering quite a bit of pain lately, but had simply favored the other side of my mouth until the pain went away all by itself. Unfortunately it looked as if Harriet might be right after all: toothaches don't simply go away, the way other aches and pains often do. They need a professional's touch to get better.

"So is she going to fix my teeth now?" I asked, speaking a little unclearly as one does when a veterinarian has her fingers jammed practically down one's throat.

"You're going to have to leave him with me," said Vena, finally dragging her eyes away from the devastated area that apparently was my mouth.

"What?" I said, aghast.

"I need to pull all these," she said, as she raked her finger along my painful teeth, in the process drawing a whimper from yours truly. "And to do that I need to sedate him, of course, and then when he wakes up I'd like to make sure he's fine before I send him home."

"But I don't want to stay here!" I said.

"It's necessary," Vena said, as if she could actually understand my heartfelt lament.

"Of course," said Odelia, immediately caving like a true wimp!

"I'm also going to draw some blood," said Vena, and proceeded to bring out a huge lawnmower!

Well, not a lawnmower, maybe, but one of those contraptions Chase likes to use in the morning to remove the stubble from his chin and cheeks.

And before I knew what was happening, she'd planted the contraption against my arm and was using it to remove my precious fur!

"Oh, my God!" Brutus cried, holding his paws up to his head in consternation.

"I can't watch this," said Harriet, turning away from the horrid procedure.

"Does it hurt, Max?" asked Dooley, the third one in the peanut gallery to make a comment.

"No, it doesn't hurt, but it's not much fun either!" I said. "Any more stupid questions?"

They all winced as they watched how Vena, with practiced ease, removed a large swath of perfectly fine fur from my arm, then plucked away the remainder and threw the whole lot into the garbage!

"Hey, I need that fur!" I said, aghast. "That's my fur! You can't just go and—"

"Just a tiny little prick," said Vena, and suddenly jabbed a needle into my arm!

"Owowow!" I cried. That wasn't a tiny prick, you liar!

"Normally I sedate them at this point," said Vena, "but since Max is always such a good boy..." She casually extracted about a pint of blood, then attached a second tube!

"Is that... blood?" asked Harriet, and promptly passed out.

"Oops," said Vena. "Yeah, this is not very pleasant, is it, Maxie, darling?"

"No, it's not!" I cried as I stared at my blood draining away into the tube.

"Harriet!" Brutus squealed. "Harriet! Say something! Doc! Harriet dropped dead! My snuggle bug just dropped dead on me! She's dead, I'm telling you. Dooooooc!"

"Harriet?" said Odelia as she rubbed Harriet's back. "Are you all right, sweetie?"

In response, Harriet merely muttered something about blood.

Vena adroitly extracted the second tube, removed the needle from my arm, then checked Harriet. She smiled. "She'll be fine. Maybe you shouldn't have brought them, Odelia. Cats are sensitive creatures, and it looks a great deal worse than it feels."

"No, it doesn't!" I said. "In fact it feels a great deal worse than it looks!"

"Since they don't know what's happening, and don't

understand, all they see is me poking their friend with a needle, so they must all be pretty upset right now."

"I'm not upset," said Dooley. "I just wonder where all that red stuff is coming from?"

"That's blood, Dooley," I said tersely. "My blood!"

"Oh," said Dooley, frowning. "You mean, Vena is a vampire?"

"Just give her a minute," said Vena, placing Harriet on a chair. "Now let's continue, shall we?" She had spilled a drop of blood on her metal operation table, and now pressed some sort of contraption against it. "Let's check his blood sugar level..." she murmured. She keenly eyed the device and nodded. "Looks good. He doesn't have diabetes."

"Diabetes!" I said.

"Now let's have a listen to his heart..." And she pressed some cold thingamabob into my chest! "Mh..." she said, listening intently at the other end of the weird-looking device, and proceeding to poke me all over my tender corpus! Finally she smiled. "No. No problems there. His heart is fine. Now let's put him on the scale."

And before I knew what was happening, she'd carried me over to a corner of her consulting room, and placed me on a big metal plate and held me in place with her gloved hand. I have to confess I wasn't giving her friendly glances. But she paid me no mind.

"Mh," she said after a moment. "He's still a little heavier than I like to see."

"I'm not heavy!" I said, indignant.

"How much do you feed him?"

"Well..." said Odelia, thinking.

Basically she feeds me however much I like to eat. As she should!

"Does he get a lot of exercise?"

"He does move around a lot," Odelia confirmed.

197

"Where am I?" asked Harriet, emerging from her malaise. "Blood!" she cried when she saw me, and immediately became woozy again. Only this time, at least, she didn't pass out on us.

"I would like him to lose at least three pounds," said Vena now, the spoilsport. "We don't want him to get diabetes, or heart disease."

"And I would like to state, for the record, that I feel perfectly fine," I said.

"You should limit his portions," said Vena, "and perhaps switch back over to the diet kibble. That seems to have done the trick last time."

"He doesn't like the diet kibble, though," said Odelia, and I gave her two paws up for coming to my defense!

"Yeah, well, that can't be helped, I'm afraid," said Vena with a truly wicked smile. "I'm going to run some more tests right now, and then later tonight I'll do the procedure."

"Thanks, Vena," said Odelia, then turned to me, still sitting on that sneaky scale. "See you later, sweetie," she said, grabbing my cheeks between her hands and pushing them together, like humans tend to do with babies and toddlers.

"Do I really have to stay here, Odelia?" I asked with a groan.

"Oh, yes, you do," she said. "You need to have this operation, Max. But I promise, you'll feel so much better afterward. No more pain. And you'll be able to chew again."

"Diet kibble," I muttered darkly.

"He won't be able to eat kibble for three weeks, though," said Vena now. "Only soft food for a while." And she proceeded to pick me up, and inject something into my back.

"Ouch!" I cried. "When is this torture ever going to stop?!"

"Just some antibiotics," she explained. "Against the infection."

What did I tell you? A visit to Vena is like a visit to a

torture chamber, or the place where that guy from *Saw* lives. Needles, needles, more needles and diet kibble!

And to add insult to injury, Harriet, Brutus and Dooley filed out of the room, giving me waves with their paws, and then Odelia closed the door and it was just me and Vena…

ABOUT NIC

Nic Saint is the pen name for writing couple Nick and Nicole Saint. They've penned novels in the romance, cat sleuth, middle grade, suspense, comedy and cozy mystery genres. Nicole has a background in accounting and Nick in political science and before being struck by the writing bug the Saints worked odd jobs around the world (including massage therapist in Mexico, gardener in Italy, restaurant manager in India, and Berlitz teacher in Belgium).

When they're not writing they enjoy Christmas-themed Hallmark movies (whether it's Christmas or not), all manner of pastry, comic books, a daily dose of yoga (to limber up those limbs), and spoiling their big red tomcat Tommy.

www.nicsaint.com

ALSO BY NIC SAINT

The Mysteries of Max
Purrfect Murder
Purrfectly Deadly
Purrfect Revenge
Box Set 1 (Books 1-3)
Purrfect Heat
Purrfect Crime
Purrfect Rivalry
Box Set 2 (Books 4-6)
Purrfect Peril
Purrfect Secret
Purrfect Alibi
Box Set 3 (Books 7-9)
Purrfect Obsession
Purrfect Betrayal
Purrfectly Clueless
Box Set 4 (Books 10-12)
Purrfectly Royal
Purrfect Cut
Purrfect Trap
Purrfectly Hidden
Purrfect Kill

Purrfect Santa
Purrfectly Flealess

Nora Steel

Murder Retreat

The Kellys

Murder Motel

Death in Suburbia

Emily Stone

Murder at the Art Class

Washington & Jefferson

First Shot

Alice Whitehouse

Spooky Times

Spooky Trills

Spooky End

Spooky Spells

Ghosts of London

Between a Ghost and a Spooky Place

Public Ghost Number One

Ghost Save the Queen

Box Set 1 (Books 1-3)

A Tale of Two Harrys

Ghost of Girlband Past

Ghostlier Things

Charleneland

Deadly Ride

Final Ride

Standalone Novels

ThrillFix

Made in the USA
San Bernardino, CA
04 August 2020

76414076R10129